Look for More Titles by Cassandra Chandler

Other Works
CRAFTING A WRITER'S LIFE: Building a Foundation

Coming Soon

The Blades of Janus
PERIHELION

The Department of Homeworld Security
Nothing to Declare

Business or Pleasure

The Department of Homeworld Security
Book Three

Cassandra Chandler

Copyright Page

This book is pure fiction. All characters, places, names, and events are products of the author's imagination or used solely in a fictitious manner. Any resemblance to any people, places, things, or events that have ever existed or will ever exist is entirely coincidental.

Business or Pleasure
The Department of Homeworld Security, Book Three
Copyright © 2016 by Cassandra Chandler
Print ISBN: 978-1-945702-34-1
Digital ISBN: 978-0-9974486-1-0

First eBook edition: June 2016
Second eBook edition: May 2017
First print edition: December 2018
10 9 8 7 6 5 4 3 2 1

cassandra-chandler.com
P.O. Box 91
Mission, Kansas 66201

Dedication

For my husband—it's always a pleasure.

Don't miss out on any of the alien action.
Subscribe to Cassandra Chandler's newsletter at
cassandra-chandler.com!

Chapter One

At six-thirty on Saturday mornings, the gym was usually deserted. It was therefore Paige's favorite workout of the week. She had already completed a few circuits on the weight machines and was enjoying being the only person using the line of treadmills as she cooled down. After the week she'd had, she needed the break from human contact.

Her playlist abruptly switched to her brother Brendan's ringtone. Damn.

Thanks to him, all she had to do to answer was tap her right earbud. He had hooked her up with technology he'd designed himself. The earbuds included tiny microphones that could pick up her voice even if she was whispering, while filtering out ambient noise and making her hands-free talking crystal clear. The phone's reception was good enough that she wondered if he was tapping into one of the secret government satellites he worked on.

Allegedly.

The downside of the awesome tech was that she felt obligated to answer every time he called her with it. She sighed, then tapped the earbud.

"Morning, bro. What's up?"

"Hey. You're at the gym, right?"

She hesitated before answering. "Yeah."

"I figured. How are you doing?"

"I'm fine, everything is fine…"

Except it really wasn't. Jim—Senator Conroy—was dead. Today's workout was as much about grief and catharsis as keeping up with her physical health. She wasn't just sad to lose the best boss she'd ever had. Senator Conroy had been a passionate visionary. He was determined to tighten environmental laws.

Her team, which consisted of her and two ever-changing temporary interns from the local college, had been working several sites in Louisiana for three years before Jim came on board, giving her renewed hope that she could make a difference. He had been in office less than a month when his plane crashed.

Maybe Brendan was just calling to check up on her.

"I'm sending someone over," he said.

She let out another sigh, deeper than the first. "Seriously? We're not even in the same state."

"I have a…friend in the area," he said. "He should be there any minute."

"How do you even know what gym I'm at?"

"Uh…"

"Don't bother answering."

Brendan was overprotective to the point of paranoia.

She had finally been able to get him to stop hiring and assigning her bodyguards by agreeing to carry a panic button with her at all times. Brendan had designed it to look like lipstick. She wasn't sure how it worked—she just knew to press the button and it would send him some sort of signal that let him know where she was and that she was in trouble.

"I've told you before, I refuse to let your work impact my life. You want to work on top secret stuff—"

"Paige—"

"—that's your business. But I'm not going to walk around with ex-military private security goons following me just to make you feel better about your life choices."

"Paige!"

Brendan never yelled. She stopped ranting.

"This isn't about me or my work," he said. "It's about you."

"What about me?"

"Whatever you're working on has caught the attention of...unsavory types."

She let out a brief laugh. "I can't even get people to believe global climate change is real, let alone that it's impacting key ecosystems. I doubt anybody sees my work as a threat, especially now that Senator Conroy is gone."

"I wish that was the case. Listen to me very carefully. I can't speak openly right now."

She snorted. Right, Brendan couldn't speak openly on

the incredibly advanced, encoded system that he had designed. She was pretty sure the government would be pissed if they ever found out she was walking around with the tech he had given her. Brendan had assured her when he set her up with her phone and panic button that no one would know about it and his *gifts* wouldn't pose a threat to national security. The last thing she wanted was to be walking around with classified technology.

As rudimentary as he claimed it to be, her calls were still supposed to be one-hundred percent unhackable. If Brendan couldn't talk freely, that meant either he had been pulled back in by the government and they were eavesdropping using the tech he had designed for them, or the much more terrifying possibility—someone was with him that Brendan deemed a threat.

"You don't need a wormhole, do you?"

That was their code for a dangerous situation they needed a miracle to get out of—like the sudden appearance of a stable wormhole. His answer would let her know if he was safe. He laughed, and some of the tension in her chest receded.

"Not in the sense you mean. You wouldn't believe... Well, anyway, I'm in a safe spot. And I'm sending someone to bring you here. We need to talk."

"I'm glad you're safe, but I'm not leaving."

"Paige—"

"If I'm on someone's radar, that means I'm onto

something. I'm not about to drop it." Whatever *it* was.

Most people would consider her overworked, but she didn't care about the long hours. She was dedicated to helping the planet. The problem with the heavy workload was that she had so many locations and projects she was tracking, she had no clue which one had pushed someone's buttons.

Brendan's call had spooked her though. She glanced around the gym, noting that several people had filtered in while they spoke. Everyone seemed absorbed in their workouts.

"I'm not telling you to abandon your work," Brendan said. "I'm saying there's more going on here than you realize. Much more. You're going to need help, whether you want it or not."

"I don't want one of your..."

A tall man stepped into the main workout room. He was pale and blond, his hair cut short on the sides and back with bangs that fell partway down his forehead. His gray T-shirt pulled tight across the most gorgeous pecs she had ever seen. His broad shoulders perfectly offset his narrow hips and accented his V figure. Tight jeans encased his long legs, all the way down to...black boots.

She rolled her eyes. He might have been able to fool her if not for the boots. Well, and the stance. The way he walked screamed military. The question at the front of her mind became—was he Brendan's guy or someone else's?

"Tell me more about this friend you're sending."

"He's tall. Looks like Thor. Not like movie-Thor, but actual *God of Lighting*-Thor."

She grinned. "And you felt safe sending him to watch over your baby sister?"

Before Brendan had made her the panic button, Paige had seduced a few of the more attractive bodyguards he tried to saddle her with. It was a great way to let off steam, but invariably had led to them wanting more of a commitment. She was already committed to her work. Still, it worked for getting them to quit and gave her fuel to tease her brother.

"Please try to take this seriously. Khel will keep you safe and explain as much as he can."

"Kel?"

"K-H-E-L. Go easy on him. He's not from around here."

"I'll make sure he feels welcome." She purred the words, wanting to make Brendan uncomfortable. He should be for intruding in her life this way—again.

"Yeah, good luck with that. And gross." Brendan laughed as if he knew something she didn't. Which wasn't that unusual. He was quiet for a moment, then said, "I love you, sis."

"I love you, too. Be safe."

"And you."

She tapped the earbud to end the call, then turned off

her music. That had been their standard wrap up to a conversation, but there was a new tension to it. The teasing had been more strained, and that pause before his, 'I love you...'

She tried to shake off the unease and focused instead on the hottie headed her way. This guy might be enough for her to chance a fling. Her body was already tingling just from watching him approach. He was scanning the room, his brows drawn together so tight they almost touched in the center of his forehead. When he reached her, he stared at her legs.

Okay, he was a leg guy. After a few moments longer than a normal person would stare, he cleared his throat and said, "Paige Sloan. I am Khel."

He cut himself off, as if he was used to saying something more than that. Probably rank and serial number.

"Khel. I am Paige Sloan," she parroted back. He didn't pick up on the teasing. If anything, he seemed reassured by her mocking response.

"Your brother has sent me to secure your safety. We must leave at once."

"My brother is not in charge of me. Nor are you. We will leave when I'm good and ready."

His mouth dropped open, then shut, then opened, then shut. Like a giant thunder-god goldfish.

She laughed. He scowled.

Right, she was supposed to take it easy on him.

"I'm almost done with my workout. Surely the world won't end if I spend another minute on the treadmill."

He stared at her feet, then looked back over the room. She thought he was checking for threats again, but then he said, "What are you all doing?"

"We're working out."

The treadmill beeped and she hit the button to turn it off. He glanced back at her as she jumped down and grabbed her towel. She felt a bead of sweat run between her cleavage and noticed how his gaze followed it. She blotted at her neck as she stepped in close.

Standing on the floor instead of the treadmill, he was even taller than she thought. She had to crane her neck back to look at him. He had that same confused scowl on his face.

"You know," she said. "Exercise?"

Nothing.

She gestured to his physique. "How do you stay in such great shape?"

"Now is not the time for questions," he said.

Eyeing him up and down, she made her voice breathy as she said, "Then I guess you can leave it to my imagination."

His gaze snapped back to hers and his lips thinned as he pressed them together. She turned and headed for the locker room, grinning as he fell in step behind her.

"We must leave at once," he said.

"Not until I shower." She pulled out her earbuds and tucked them into the back pocket of her workout shorts next to her phone.

"This *shower* can not be more important than your safety. The longer we delay, the more opportunities our enemies will have to attack."

He sounded like one of Brendan's cosplaying friends. For a moment, she wondered if the whole thing was an elaborate charade.

"If this is Brendan playing a practical joke on me, I'm going to kick his ass when I see him."

"That is outside the scope of my orders."

She rolled her eyes and pushed open the door to the women's locker room. Khel followed her in.

"Um, Khel?"

"Yes?"

He stopped when she did, glancing around the room. If this *was* a joke, he was taking it pretty seriously. He also didn't seem disturbed at all at being in a women's locker room.

"You're not supposed to be in here," she said.

"I go where you go."

He fixed his gaze on her, clear blue eyes boring through her. She decided to have a little fun.

"Okay."

She gripped the bottom of her sports bra—the only top

she wore while working out—and pulled it over her head, smirking. His gaze flicked to her chest, then back to her face. He didn't even look like he was *trying* not to look.

She wasn't used to men ignoring her body. She worked hard to be attractive. It helped her self-esteem and prevented her from having to endure lonely nights when she felt like a little company. She was *stacked* and never had trouble finding men who considered the red hair and blue eyes a bonus.

Khel didn't flinch, didn't twitch, didn't alter his expression or body language one iota. He just stared at her. At her *face*.

"Proceed," he said.

Wow. That pinged her ego. She turned around and walked to her locker.

Whatever. He wasn't into her. It had happened before and would happen again. She had to admit she was disappointed, though. He was gorgeous and it had been a while since she'd indulged in a carnal weekend with anyone.

She finished stripping and threw her workout clothes into a bag, then grabbed her toiletries and slid on some flip-flops. Khel stood at the end of the row of lockers, looking left and right. Good thing the locker room was empty.

As she walked past him to the showers, he started after her. The thought of him watching her shower with that cold stare set her teeth on edge.

"Not so fast." She turned around and planted a hand on his chest.

Heat and warmth flooded into her. His chest was rock-hard, and damn, those shoulders. She could grab onto them and do all sorts of things...

Khel sucked in a huge breath and held it. Okay. That was a response. But she wasn't into mixed signals. She pulled her hand away.

"This is as far as you go," she said.

"I am ordered to see to your safety."

"I don't care what my brother says."

He bristled. "I don't take orders from a...Brendan."

A Brendan?

She finished his original sentence in her head. *He doesn't take orders from a civilian.*

Shit. Khel was military, but not 'ex'. Brendan had told her he was taking a break from his projects. He must have been pulled back in—and somehow she was swept up with it.

Yes, technically they both worked for the government, and yes, she had received a certain level of clearance based on whatever the hell he was working on. But she had her own life, her own job, her own cause.

She would not be controlled.

Chapter Two

"I don't know who you work for, but you can tell them to go straight to hell."

This Earthling was infuriating. Khel had told her she was in danger and the first thing she had done was strip naked.

His mental programming session for going planetside on Earth had been necessarily brief. It had given him access to several languages and basic cultural functions. He must be misunderstanding the term *shower*. It was impossible that she saw cleansing her body as more important than her safety.

She turned around and walked into a room covered in small square tiles. He followed her. At least here there were fewer ambush points. She walked up to a wall with several protruding knobs, hoses, and small hooks. She hung the bag she had taken from her locker near two of the knobs, then turned them.

Water poured out from the hose above her. Her breath hitched, and she made some adjustments, then let out a sigh.

The extravagance of it... Potable water used to cleanse

their bodies? He hadn't actually believed the programming until he saw this. So many planets struggled to generate enough water to sustain life. Earthlings *bathed* in it.

As a soldier for the Coalition of planets, Khel had access to technology that made things like showers unnecessary. Between the cleansing properties of his uniform and the regen bed where he slept, his body was maintained for him. He only needed to remove his uniform for eliminations. The genetic engineers who created Sadirians hadn't been able to craft a more civilized way to deal with those bodily functions. Yet.

Paige turned to face him, a grimace pulling the edges of her lips. Leaning back, she let the water pour over her head. The bright copper of her hair changed color, darkening to a burgundy-laced brown.

She pulled a tube from her bag hanging on the wall and squeezed out a semi-liquid substance. Lifting her hands to her head, she worked the gel into her hair, creating a thick lather. She leaned her head back again, letting the water pour over her, rinsing her clean.

Her eyes were almost Sadirian in their size and shape. The similarities ended there. Her nose was short and pert, her lips full, and her cheekbones muted. The bright color to her hair was nearly identical to a shade that was popular in quadrant seven, but that style was completed with gold eyes and bronzed skin. Paige's skin was even paler than his and her eyes were a slightly darker blue.

Sadirians were strong, but their muscles tended to not show through their skin. His people appeared smooth. Their arms and legs barely had variance in shape, straight lines preferred aesthetically. The same held true for their torsos.

Khel was different. He was a glitch.

Tall didn't begin to describe him. He was monstrously huge, his body reacting with the regen bed that stimulated his muscles during sleep cycles to turn him into a gargantuan specimen. The genetic engineers who created him had studied his body for years after he reached maturity before letting him begin his life as a soldier, trying to figure out where they had gone wrong.

Even without the muscles, his bone structure made him useless. Space stations and ships were often small and used every inch effectively. The *Arbiter* was one of the few ships in the fleet that had mechanical tunnels large enough for him to squeeze through.

Paige was small and compact. She could easily fit through those tight places. She was as short as a standard Sadirian, but her body seemed composed entirely of curves. Her waist was narrow and her hips broad. Her legs were heavily muscled, as was the rest of her. And her breasts were larger than any he had ever seen. He had a bizarre urge to heft them and feel their weight in his hands. They appeared soft.

She pulled another tube from her bag and squeezed out

more gelatinous matter. She put her hands to her breasts, massaging them as she created more lather. Trails of suds ran down her stomach, catching in the fine curls between her legs.

Something shifted in him. Heat was gathering low in his abdomen. Blood was pooling in his penis.

"For someone in such a hurry a minute ago, you sure are getting off on watching me shower." She ran her hands along her arms.

"Getting off of what?"

Turning, she massaged the lather into the supple skin of her buttocks. He wanted to touch her hips, to hold them firmly, pull her up against him—

Cygnus X, why would that even occur to him? The thought made the tightening in his penis worse, his jeans chafing. He took several deep breaths, trying to will his body to calm. It had worked the few times his body had reacted to other Sadirians.

It wasn't working with this Earthling.

She turned back to face him, letting the water pour over her shoulders. Her grimace had turned to a grin. Her hands traced the water's path down her stomach toward...

"Look out!" she yelled.

His gaze snapped back to her face. Her eyes were wide as she stared at something above him. He leapt out of the way just before a Tau Ceti dropped to the floor with a loud clang.

Cybernetic enhancements. Of course.

It looked like an average human male—light brown hair falling over its face and dressed in Earth clothing. The Tau Ceti truly were doing their best to fit in as they invaded the planet.

Khel didn't waste a moment. He lashed out with a kick that should have caught the Tau Ceti in the ribs. The strike didn't connect. The cyborg was too quick. Khel swung his fist, feinting to one side to draw it closer. He managed to land a blow to the side of its head. Better.

Before he could follow up, Paige leapt onto the cyborg's back. She wrapped her legs around its ribs and one arm around its neck. It reached toward her to pull her off, giving Khel the opening he needed.

He punched the Tau Ceti with all his strength, catching it in its side just below its armpit. The cyborg screeched as the nerve cluster undoubtedly sent waves of pain through its body. A follow-up strike should take it down.

Paige wasn't done with it, though. She had one of those tubes in her hand and squeezed its contents into the Tau Ceti's eyes before Khel could attack again.

The noise it made was horrifying. It clawed at its face, jerking from side to side trying to shake Paige loose. Moons, what kind of chemicals did humans use to clean themselves that were so easily weaponized?

Khel maneuvered behind the Tau Ceti, then grabbed Paige and pulled her off. The cyborg turned toward them briefly and hissed, revealing the set of long, sharp canines that grew from the roof of its mouth, normally hidden behind its regular teeth. It leapt over their heads, landing— and sticking—on the wall before scurrying around a corner. Khel doubted it would attack again immediately.

"What *the fuck* was that?" Paige yelled.

"An enemy. We must leave."

"No shit."

He followed as she ran to her locker.

"I want answers, Khel."

"I can explain once we've reached safety."

"Not going to work for me. Talk as I dress." She began quickly drying her body.

Her brother had been clear in his instructions. *Don't tell Paige about aliens until they reached Khel's ship.* Without proof, Brendan was convinced his sister would ignore their warning and refuse to leave. Khel hoped the Tau Ceti's attack was proof enough.

"Our attacker is from Tau Ceti," Khel said.

Paige shimmied into a pair of jeans, then pulled a dark green T-shirt over her head. "Tau Ceti, as in the star? You're saying that guy was an alien."

"Yes. And it has undoubtedly reported our location to others of its kind."

"*It?*"

"A cyborg."

"Great. A saber-toothed cyborg gecko." Her hair

dripped on the floor as she pulled on her socks and slipped her feet into a pair of shoes.

"Frog." When she glanced up at him, Khel said, "Your brother has been referring to them as *vampire space frogs.*"

She snorted and shook her head. "Sounds like Brendan."

She stood and pulled her hair back from her face, securing it with an elastic band. She stuffed everything into her backpack and closed the locker door. "And what are you?"

"I am Sadirian."

"This is so messed up." She swung her backpack over her shoulder and headed for the exit.

She didn't say anything until they were outside of the gym, the sun shining down on them and the air thick with moisture. The bright light would hinder the Tau Ceti's ability to see. Their eyes were too delicate for ocular implants and their homeworld existed in perpetual twilight.

"My apartment isn't far," she said.

She started past him, but he moved to block her way.

"That's the first place they'll look. We need to get to my ship. We'll be safe there."

"As in spaceship?" She rolled her eyes again. "Brendan must be beside himself with joy. Is that where he is now?"

"He's on the *Arbiter*. It's in orbit currently. My vessel is a smaller scouting ship. It can take us there."

"I'm not leaving the planet with you," she said. "This is insane! I can't believe I even just said that."

He grabbed her elbow, but stopped himself from urging her to walk. The look in her eyes promised violence. He couldn't refrain from admiring her confidence.

"Listen closely, Paige. The Tau Ceti want you. Not dead, but alive. Otherwise, we would both be vapor by now. And *you do not want them to capture you.* Trust me on that point, if nothing else."

She fidgeted, pressing her lips together. When she stilled, she was closer to him. He wasn't sure she was even aware of it, but *he* was. And of the softness of her skin beneath his hand.

"Why me?" Her voice was small. For the first time, she looked afraid.

He stepped closer, gripping her other elbow. If the Tau Ceti came back, he would be able to shield her better. And the proximity…was pleasant.

"Brendan believes your work is somehow threatening their plan for Earth. We've already lost a listening station over this, and they were willing to shoot down one of your planes."

"Wait… What?" Her eyes filled with tears. "What plane?"

He didn't want her to break down. They were conspicuous enough, standing still on the sidewalk as others passed them by. But he had already seen how intractable she could be.

"Senator Conroy's plane. That's how we knew that you were a target—and probably why they want you alive. As the only remaining human who worked with him in this area, they'll want to determine what you know and who you've spoken to about it."

Paige blew out her breath forcefully, and the tears he'd been preparing himself for vanished along with any sign of her fear. A muscle along her cheek twitched. The look he had taken as threatening before was nothing compared to this.

Murderous rage. If he gave her a disintegrator, he had no doubt she would use it. And the way she had attacked the cyborg, completely naked and armed with nothing more than soap…

She smacked his hands away, then grabbed *his* elbow, pulling him in step beside her.

"Where are we going?" he asked.

"We're going to my office to find out what these bastards are really after. They can't want me specifically. I don't have the clearance to be a threat to anyone. Jim—the senator—was the one with power. Like you said, what I have is knowledge. And copies of that knowledge are where I work."

"My orders are to protect you and bring you safely to the *Arbiter*."

"From what you've told me, my entire planet is in danger. How am I supposed to ignore that?"

She was putting the safety of her planet before herself. Admirable, especially considering Brendan had informed Khel that she had never received formal training or indoctrination related to protecting herself or others. She would make a fine soldier for the Coalition, if she could learn to follow orders.

It was all the more impressive that her personal choice was to risk herself to help others. And fearlessly—without the aid of chemicals to control her emotions.

What must it be like to take action based on one's own choices rather than orders or conditioning?

Khel followed his training, but didn't rely on the Coalition drugs *Balance* or *Coupling* to maintain emotional and mental equilibrium. His work aboard the *Arbiter* kept him satisfied. Work that was about to change radically.

The plan General Serath—Adam—had laid out before Khel left on his mission plagued him. Convincing the Coalition to stop using *Balance* to keep the population peaceful—giving citizens more autonomy—would cause widespread chaos throughout the galaxy.

Khel had no illusions about the violence and suffering that would result as septillions of sentients learned how to interact on their own. He understood there was corruption within the Coalition, but wasn't sure he was ready to assist with such upheaval. Surely there was another way.

His thoughts were interrupted as a large transport approached them. Paige waved at it, walking toward the street. The vehicle stopped next to them and a set of doors opened with a pneumatic whoosh. She stepped aboard and turned back to him.

"I'm going," she said. "You can come along or not. The choice is yours."

He hesitated briefly before following.

Chapter Three

Paige led Khel to the back of the bus and sat near the window. He filled the space at her side, his sheer size a comforting presence. It would be hard for any "Tau Ceti" to see her past Khel, let alone attack her.

Space frogs. *Cyborg* space frogs.

She had to be dreaming. That would explain Khel too, with his delicious physique and intriguing mix of hot-and-cold reactions to her. Stripping hadn't seemed to register with him at all. But showering in front of him...

He had watched her like he wanted to devour her. Before the stupid space frog attacked, she was getting ready to invite him to dinner.

Space frogs. *Killer* space frogs.

She shook her head, as if that would help her process things. No matter how much she wanted to not-believe, she couldn't discount the evidence of her own senses. She had seen that man cling to the tile of the locker room walls with nothing but his hands and feet. She had felt the mix of steel and flesh when she attacked him. She had seen his menacing fangs.

These aliens had crashed Jim's plane on purpose. If she

hadn't volunteered to help out with a colleague's cleanup site—which turned out to be much more involved than she was led to believe—she would have been on that plane with him. And now the Tau Ceti wanted her—alive.

She shivered at what Khel had implied earlier. Brendan wasn't the only scifi fan in the family. She had seen plenty of movies that gave her horrifying possibilities of what capture might entail. She had also seen tons of movies that showed what might happen to the planet after aliens invaded.

Not on her watch.

"I'm the project lead." She wiped at her eyes and sniffed. "And I'm between interns at the moment. Jim and I—the senator—we were talking about bringing in more full-time staff. I've been buried in paperwork for the past few weeks, trying to figure out how to bring my new team up to speed as quickly as possible with the resources I was supposed to get."

She snorted and shook her head. No team. No champion. It was just her and Khel. She reached over and put her hand on the fist he was resting on his thigh.

"What are you doing?" he asked.

"Trying to hold your hand."

He stared down at her with those cold blue eyes. She had seen the fire in them, white-hot. He would probably be amazing in bed—if he could let go of some of his repression. She pried open his fist, then interlaced their fingers and set their hands back on his leg.

"What is the significance of this?" he asked.

"Reassurance, closeness… Don't you *Sadirians* seek physical comfort from each other?"

"Our culture is different. We have moved beyond the need to obey our base instincts."

"Base instincts?" She snorted again. "That's just sad. No hugging? Kissing?"

His lips pulled into a thin line as he looked over the people on the bus again.

"No sex?"

He glanced over to her, then turned away. "Some Sadirians still seek physical pairing. Most are content to use *Coupling*."

"What's that?"

"A drug that takes the body through the stages of arousal to culmination. It's generally used alone, but some Sadirians prefer to use it with a partner."

"You only have sex while you're on drugs?"

He glared at her. "I don't use *Coupling*."

"Okay. You just made it sound like people only have sex if they're on it."

"That's correct."

"So wait… You've never… I mean…"

She couldn't even say it. It was so outlandish. This amazingly hot guy—with a body she'd love to turn into a carnal carnival—had never had sex. Even with himself.

She shook her head. "Seems like a waste of natural resources to me."

His scowl deepened.

He lifted their entwined hands and said, "Is this meeting your need?"

"What need?"

"For physical comfort."

He turned back toward the other passengers. She followed his gaze to a young couple snuggling a few seats ahead.

She was tempted to ask for more, but that would be taking advantage. Instead she said, "I'm fine."

He extricated his hand and put his arm over her shoulders. He pulled her tight against his side, surprising her with the gentleness of the gesture. For someone who wasn't used to touch, he was a pretty good side-hugger.

"Is this better?" he asked.

"Yeah. Much."

He was sitting perfectly straight. His muscles were rigid against her. Did he even know how to relax?

That was a question for another time.

"Now I understand why you were so comfortable with me getting naked," she said.

"On stations and ships, citizens and soldiers alike live in close proximity. Viewing each other's bodies is a common occurrence."

"On my planet, nudity often precedes sex. We take it a

bit more seriously."

"Noted. I'll be sure to update our base-line cultural overview to that effect."

She nestled against him, resting her hand on his thigh. He sucked in a breath and held it. Poor guy. Touch was obviously something he wasn't comfortable with. But he was doing it to help her feel better.

"Thanks," she said.

"I am merely performing my duty."

"I seriously doubt snuggling was part of your orders."

"*Snuggling.* No." He glanced at her briefly before returning to his continual survey of their surroundings.

"Tell me more about the Tau Ceti. What do they want with Earth?"

"They want something from Earthlings."

"I'm guessing this isn't an *Earth Girls are Easy* kind of situation based on what happened in the locker room."

"I don't understand."

"It's a movie about aliens who come to Earth basically looking for sex."

He let out a brief snort. So, he was capable of finding things amusing. Very good.

"Don't knock it till you've tried it," she said.

He stared at her for several long moments. She held his gaze, letting herself smirk as she cocked an eyebrow at him. If he was interested in experimenting...

"They're siphoning off hormones humans generate

when they're happy," he said.

Well, that killed the moment.

She remembered the sharp fangs in the Tau Ceti from the locker room and Brendan's nickname for the aliens. *Vampire* space frogs. A chill ran down her spine. She turned away and looked out the window as she pulled herself together.

Shit. This was real. And these things were feeding on people.

"When they...collect...what does it do to the person?"

"We aren't sure. We can only guess it disrupts the Earthling's body chemistry, leading to sadness or depression."

Great. As if there wasn't enough of that in the world already.

She took a deep breath and blew it out through pursed lips. "I still don't see how I'm involved."

"The Tau Ceti have set up at least one base of operations on Earth. We were able to intercept a record of some samples you took that match the ecosystem on Tau Ceti 6—their homeworld."

"How different from Earth's natural ecosystems are we talking?"

"Different enough. Tau Ceti 6 is warmer than Earth and covered in dense foliage and moisture. It's similar to an equatorial swamp on Earth, but there are key chemicals the Tau Ceti need to thrive. Those chemicals are not harmonious to indigenous lifeforms."

"You've got to be kidding me."

It was bad enough that she had to protect the Earth from humans, but now she had to fight to get vampire space frogs to stop messing up the environment, too?

"Where were the samples taken?" she asked.

"We weren't able to determine that."

"Well, then, let's see if we can figure it out."

The bus pulled up to the curb near the office building where she worked. She and Khel stood and made their way back out into the sweltering day. As the bus pulled away from them, she glanced around. It was creepy thinking that any of the people walking by could actually be aliens.

"Is this what you really look like?" she asked.

"What do you mean?"

"You look like an Earthling. Is it a disguise?"

"No, this is how I was made."

"Made?"

His lips thinned again. "Sadirians are genetically engineered."

"Oh wow. Please tell me everyone looks like you where you're from."

"They don't." The words were clipped and he was glaring at her again.

"Okay. Sensitive topic."

She headed toward her office building and he followed.

Somehow, she had to get Khel past Harry, the security guard at the front desk. Since barely anyone used the building on weekends, Harry was always the only one on duty. Budget restrictions.

The building didn't house anything that was deemed classified, so a single guard paid for by the building's management worked for everyone. Her group of environmental scientists had one floor, and the others were occupied by various businesses.

Nobody on Earth thought her work was important. She couldn't believe people from outer space were so interested.

"The process isn't infallible," Khel said.

He spoke so abruptly that she had trouble tracking him at first.

"What process?"

"Genetic engineering. Mistakes are made."

"Is that what happened with the Tau Ceti?"

They looked like the same species to her. Hell, all the aliens looked like humans, until they started to do things like stick to walls.

"No, the Tau Ceti are a different species entirely. Their engineers have been highly successful in crafting individuals who appear Sadirian. The Tau Ceti who attacked you looks much more Sadirian than I."

"Seriously?"

"I'm considered an unsuccessful specimen."

She laughed at that. Hard and long.

"I'm sorry," she said. "You're serious? You realize on Earth you're considered absolutely gorgeous, right?"

His scowl deepened.

"I'm not teasing. You could have your pick of partners." Hell, he could have her in a heartbeat. "That's not why you haven't experienced *Coupling*, is it?"

She wanted to know why this was such a sensitive subject for him. The thought of him being rejected because of how he looked was baffling and tragic. His society must have really different standards of beauty.

"I've had opportunities. The *Arbiter* is populated entirely by glitches like myself."

And there it was—the real reason it was an issue for him. A label conveniently marking him and others like him as being of less value. *Glitches*.

"I don't like that word," she said.

He paused briefly. "Neither do I."

She reached out and held his hand, smiling when he looked down at her. He smiled back. It was over so fast, she thought she might have imagined it. She hoped she hadn't.

Chapter Four

Bypassing the security guard was a disturbingly simple matter. He appeared to be sleeping when they arrived. They managed to slip past him unnoticed. If one of Khel's soldiers had been caught sleeping on duty...

He wasn't certain what the penalty would be. It had never happened before.

Earthlings certainly seemed to be relaxed about many things. Like Paige with her constant touches and talk of *Coupling*—sex. Trapped in a small lift with her, she once again turned to her favorite line of inquiry.

"Does *Coupling* enhance sex for the people who use it?"

"I don't know," he said.

"Right. Sorry. But you've never been curious? Even when you had those opportunities you mentioned?"

He had never been curious. At least, not aboard the *Arbiter*. But the skin of his thigh still tingled from her touch, his penis remaining half-engorged since the moment they had met, it seemed. Holding her against his side had felt peaceful, even while it set parts of him stirring. Khel was bewildered by the effect she was having on him—physically, mentally, and emotionally.

Primarily physically.

"Do you ever think about anything but sex?" he asked.

"Of course I do. But sex is one of my best coping mechanisms for stress, and in case you hadn't noticed, this is a pretty stressful situation. Plus I've read way too many books with elevator sex scenes. Even without our earlier conversation, riding in an elevator with a guy like you would have me thinking through scenarios."

A guy like him? His cheeks heated, a strange prickling sensation spreading over his skin.

How would someone go about having sex in an elevator? He was too tall to lay prone on the floor. If she took off her jeans, she could wrap her legs around his waist and he could hold her in place by pinning her to the wall...

Where in the name of the Solar Cross had that thought come from? His penis stiffened further and he shifted his weight to try to be more comfortable. Her gaze slid down his body, and she smirked at him again.

Infuriating. Exasperating.

What if she held onto the railing while he took her from behind...

A bell sounded.

"This is where we get off." She grinned and waggled her eyebrows up and down. It was strangely comical, and he laughed.

Laughing. He had done it with his comrades, of course, during late nights of games and after their many victories. This one was different. Smaller, yet deeper. It made his chest feel less heavy.

He needed to focus.

Paige threaded her hand through his arm, locking their elbows, and leaned into his side. "Let's go."

The doors opened and she led him onto a semi-lit level of the building. The dim environment would be perfect for Tau Ceti vision. He pulled himself more to attention.

"My office is this way."

He followed her to a small room lined with tables and a desk. Every horizontal surface was covered with papers. She dropped her bag on the floor.

"What is this?" he asked.

"My filing system."

"This isn't a system. This is chaos."

"Carefully contained chaos. Have a seat."

She spun her chair toward him. Khel doubted he would fit.

"I prefer to stand guard at the door."

"I don't know what I'm looking for. I need you to go over this data with me." She patted the back of the chair. Reluctantly, he scrunched himself into the seat. She leaned over his shoulder and whispered in his ear. "That wasn't so bad, was it?"

Sitting in the chair, no. Her warm breath on his neck

was another matter. He shifted in his seat again. She patted his shoulder and grinned at him.

She started to go through papers, setting stacks in front of him. "These are the most recent topographic maps. Aerial photos from the last few years. I've been focusing on the impact of climate change on nearby wetlands."

"Is any of this data available digitally?"

She shook her head. "I know it's ironic, but we haven't had funding to upgrade our systems and still rely way too much on paper. We recycle everything, at least. My interns were supposed to scan these into the computers eventually, but we were always too busy getting out in the field and collecting samples, running tests... I figured I'd get around to entering it all in the system eventually."

Khel nodded. "Then the Tau Ceti have no idea how much you know. They could easily hack your computer systems, but since you only have hard copies, they'll have to come here. They'll want to know what you've figured out."

"I haven't figured out anything. But we're going to change that."

She turned around and bent over her desk to reach some papers that were stacked on the very back corner. Her jeans hugged the curves of her backside. He was already reaching for her hips when she straightened. He quickly diverted to the papers in front of him instead. She didn't seem to have noticed. Leaning against the desk, she pulled one side of her lower lip between her teeth and started to read.

Putting his attention into their work was an excellent idea. Maybe it could push the thoughts of her out of his mind. Time passed where the only sound in the room was the rustling of paper.

What was happening to him? His thoughts kept straying back to her.

She was holding up remarkably well. He still couldn't believe she had attacked a Tau Ceti soldier. One with cybernetic enhancements. True, she hadn't known what she was fighting, but she refused to let Khel face the threat alone—even though she was naked.

Paige naked.

Their conversation had made him start to think, to question ways he had perceived the world and himself. His place in it, how he interacted with others.

He had been approached before by Sadirians interested in using *Coupling* with him. He had never been tempted in the least. The idea had frankly been off-putting. But thinking of Paige, with her soft curves and steel will—

"I think I found something."

She placed a map in front of him, then turned around and sat in his lap. He let out a grunt.

"I'm not that heavy," she said. "Sheesh."

Her attention was on the sheets of paper in her hands, which was good. His grunt hadn't been about her weight.

She was sitting snug up against his erection, that beautiful backside pressing against him. Every time she moved even an iota, he felt it reverberate through his entire body.

"Are you okay? You sound like you're about to hyperventilate." She looked at him over her shoulder. "Oh sorry. I forgot you don't like to touch."

She started to stand, but he grabbed her hips to hold her in place.

"It's okay," he grated. He stopped himself from adding, *I want more.*

The concern on her face slowly softened into something else. A slight smile, not quite the smirk she'd been taunting him with since they met. She cleared her throat and turned back to her papers, holding a bit more still, thank the stars.

"These are the numbers from the testing we did last year in some swampland we're watching closely." She held up another sheet of paper next to it. "These are the numbers from this year. I don't know how much of this you understand, but I can tell you this is really weird."

He didn't need her to explain. He could see for himself. The numbers matched the samples that Brendan and Kira had told Adam about.

"These are the samples we're looking for," Khel said. "Where did you find them?"

The look on her face was not encouraging. She set aside the papers and started pointing at the map she had placed in front of him.

"The results are the same for samples we gathered here, here, here…"

She pointed at various spots on the map. Over and over again, the range covering a staggering amount of territory.

Khel leaned forward. Without even thinking about it, he wrapped one arm around her waist to keep her steady.

The geography of the area was filled with swamp dotted by small lakes. All connected through the same waterways. He shook his head.

"This isn't a base," he said. "This is a breeding ground. The Tau Ceti are creating spawning pools."

Chapter Five

Paige didn't need Khel to tell her how bad that was. She was very aware of how destructive it could be when an invasive species was introduced. The Tau Ceti were working to gain a foothold on Earth and she had no idea how to stop them.

"We must get this information to Adam," Khel said.

"Who's that?"

"My commanding officer. Measures will be taken."

She felt the faintest glimmer of relief. It was quickly overshadowed by her experience and knowledge. Introducing another species to take out an already invading species...

"I know you're working with Brendan and that makes me trust you—partly. But I have to ask, Khel. Are you the good guys? Will you really help Earth, or are you just making room for your own people to come in and exploit our planet?"

He stared at her intently. Then he looked away. Not a good sign.

"The Coalition has designated Earth as a preserved planet. It's supposed to be protected."

"*Supposed* to be?"

"We've discovered some issues recently."

"Like vampire space frog issues?"

"Possibly worse."

Great.

"What are we going to do about it?" she asked.

Somehow, Khel didn't feel like a bodyguard. He felt like a partner. Maybe because he was actually listening to her instead of trying to control her.

"To begin, get you to my ship," he said. "Adam will need the information we've discovered to create the best course of action."

Khel rose, lifting her from his lap. He stood close, resting his hands on her arms.

"What about Earth authorities? Don't you have a secret connection to our government leaders or something?"

"That would be a very bad idea."

"This is *our* planet. We need to be able to help decide how to protect it."

"Earth isn't ready."

So much for being partners. She pulled away from him. "Why do you get to decide that?"

"Because we've seen what happens when planets as rich in resources as Earth are given a seat at the Coalition table too soon. The leaders want access to technology, and they arrange trade after trade until their planet is as barren and stripped as all the others in the Coalition."

"Then help us. Educate us. Limit us, when necessary, but at least give us a voice."

"You sound just like your brother."

She rolled her eyes.

"It's already happening, Paige. Brendan and Adam are setting it up. Not necessarily with government leaders, but we're starting to approach individuals that we think can handle it. It's early, but we're forming a First Contact council for Earth."

"Oh. Well…good."

"Brendan wants you on it to represent environmental issues."

She snorted. Yeah, right. Paige Sloan in charge of helping aliens make sure nobody messed up the Earth. Maybe even teaching them how to manage resources on the other planets in their "Coalition" and restore the environments they had stripped bare.

Wait…

"Seriously?"

A thrill of excitement shot through her. All she had ever wanted to do was protect Earth. Now she knew that there were threats to her homeworld beyond her imaginings, other planets that needed healing—and she might be able to help.

"It will only happen if we survive," Khel said. "Come on."

He opened the door to her office a crack and peered

out, then closed it again.

Paige almost bounced off his back. "I thought we were leaving."

"The guard is patrolling."

Crap.

"I didn't know he even did that."

She glanced around the small space, looking for a place to hide. Having the furniture pressed against the walls helped prevent avalanches from all the reports she had to process, but it didn't make for good hiding places. Why hadn't management stopped with all the printouts already? They were supposed to be environmentalists, for crying out loud.

"He'll be here in moments," Khel said. "I can incapacitate him."

"Absolutely not!"

Khel stared at her expectantly. She didn't know what to do. She worked plenty of Saturdays and could easily explain away her presence. Harry would probably even believe that she had forgotten to sign in. But Khel wasn't authorized to be in the building. As laid back as Harry was, he'd have to call it in.

Paige grabbed Khel by his arms and swung him around till he was standing in front of her chair. Then she pressed on his shoulders. He sat and stared at her expectantly.

Here goes nothing.

She knelt on his lap, then grabbed the back of his neck

and pulled him to her for a kiss. At least, that was the plan. He was too quick for her and angled his head away.

"What are you doing?" he asked.

"Coming up with an excuse for why you're in my office. We don't have time to explain to Harry why you're here and you don't have clearance."

"Harry?"

"The guard. If we can convince him we snuck in for a little office nookie, he'll leave us alone."

"I highly doubt—"

She pressed a finger to his lips, then ran it over their satin surface. "This is Earth. You need to start thinking like an Earthling."

His gaze bored into her, but then he grabbed her face with his strong hands, pulling her down to him. His lips brushed hers stiffly at first, but then softened as he followed her lead.

She burrowed her fingers in his hair, nipping his lips, sucking one and then the other into her mouth. He groaned and she couldn't help but smile. His hips started to move. She slid her tongue into his mouth and he froze for a moment. She explored him cautiously, giving him time to adjust. He didn't need long.

His tongue started to dance with hers, testing, teasing. He pulled her hair free from its ponytail holder and let it fall around her shoulders. He deepened the kiss, his lips massaging hers as his hands slid down to her hips. He leaned forward, pressing their chests together, his fingers tightening their grip.

"Ahem."

They both jumped at the sound behind them. Right, Harry. She had forgotten why they started making out in the first place.

"Harry! Hi," she said, shifting to sit in Khel's lap. His dick was pressing against her ass and she felt her eyes widen. "I…um…"

Right. The plan. She used her best *caught in the act* expression and did everything but bat her eyelashes.

"I just brought my friend by to show him my office."

"That right?" Harry said. "Forgot to sign in, though."

"About that… I sort of didn't want my boss to know I was here today *with someone.*"

"Mmm-hmm."

She was actually sweating. Khel's body had gone rigid beneath her, and not just in his crotch. She could feel the coiled energy in him, waiting to spring. Harry was a nice guy just doing his job. He didn't deserve to be 'incapacitated'.

"Might want to use the conference room down the hall. More table space." Harry winked at them, then was all business again. "Make sure you check in with me at the desk before you leave."

He exited the office, pulling the door shut behind him. Paige let out a deep breath.

"I can't believe that worked. I mean, it always works in my favorite romance novels, but—"

She stopped when she turned back to Khel. He hadn't relaxed at all. He was gripping the armrests of her chair so tight—

Snap.

"Oops," she said.

He kept staring at her while he held up the broken piece of chair. She carefully peeled his fingers off of it so she could toss it on the floor under her desk. There was nowhere for him to gracefully rest his arm, so she planted his hand on her hip. He sucked in a breath and held it from the looks of things.

"What do I do?" he asked.

"I don't understand the question."

"To make it go away."

"To make... Oh."

Her eyes must be bugging out of her head. The thick mass of his erection was pressing against his jeans in what had to be a really uncomfortable position.

"Let me help you."

She undid his jeans to try to let things straighten themselves out on their own without realizing...he went commando.

Chapter Six

Paige wouldn't stop staring at his erection, which was making the situation worse. Khel felt her gaze like a caress. His penis jerked on its own in response. Why wouldn't his body obey him?

He closed his eyes and willed the erection to go away. Tried to think of anything but the softness of her lips on his, the warmth of her tongue in his mouth.

His penis twitched again.

"It won't stop," he said.

"I can see that. Wow, can I see that."

He glared at her. "What do I do?"

"Haven't you ever... Of course you haven't." She let out a sigh. "You've never even had morning wood?"

"Morning wood?"

"You know, a stiffy in the morning? Wake up at attention?"

"The regen bed I sleep in would address that. It maintains our bodies, scans and treats us for illness and disease, and stimulates our muscles to keep us fit and ready for duty."

"You're certainly ready for duty." She grinned at him.

"Paige! Help me."

"Sorry." Her expression softened. "No wonder you were confused by the gym. You guys could make a fortune selling those regen beds on Earth. Work out while you sleep."

She shifted on his lap, reminding him of the fullness of her hip in his hand. Her breasts would be infinitely softer. He tightened his grip as he tried to marshal his thoughts.

He should have followed orders to the letter and taken her to his ship any way he could. He had disobeyed, and now his body and mind were doing the same to him.

"You've really never had a hard-on for someone before?" she asked.

"I've had reactions, but was always able to control them. It never took more than a few minutes of quiet distraction."

But his reaction had never been this intense. He had never tried to calm his body while he had the taste of someone on his lips—the lingering memory of their body pressed against him fueling his reaction.

"I can't function this way," he said. "How do I make it go away?"

"Uh…" Her gaze dropped to his erection again and she licked her lips.

Adam had alluded to things that Evelyn taught him about how Earthlings coupled. Khel wondered just how creative they were in using various parts of their bodies to stimulate each other.

"You can always jerk off," Paige said.

"Idioms, Paige."

She sighed and took his hand from her hip. He reluctantly allowed it. Then she wrapped his fingers around his erection.

"What are you doing?"

"Showing you how to do it. You just grip yourself and...pump."

His hand felt awkward on his flesh. It was much better where her hand touched his. He wanted something, but he wasn't sure what. More of her touch, more of those amazing kisses. Thinking of it, he realized he had felt a pull toward her from the very beginning.

When Adam had returned to the *Arbiter* with Evelyn, Khel thought the General had lost his mind.

Things changed.

"Paige, I want..." He wasn't sure what. He didn't have words for what he felt.

She had seemed interested in him from the beginning as well, but he hadn't known how to respond. He still didn't. But he *wanted*. That was the one thing that was clear. He wanted her.

She sighed, then slid his hand away and replaced it with her own. The first touch sent currents of electric stimulation along his nerve endings. Every cell in his body seemed to be focused on her slight hand wrapped around him. She gripped him tight, then began to move.

"Paige," her name was a primal moan. The energy in his body was pooling low, centering on his shaft in her cool fingers.

"The regen beds have cured all disease among your people?" she asked.

"Yes." The word was drawn out as he closed his eyes and gasped.

"And I assume you've been inoculated against everything on Earth. With all your advanced technology."

"It was…thoroughly studied…"

"Yes or no, Khel."

She squeezed his penis tighter.

"Yes." His breath was coming faster. He heard a loud crack and realized he had torn the other armrest from her chair.

They both stared at it for a moment, then she swatted it from his hand. It clattered onto the floor. She slid from his lap, kneeling in front of him.

"What are you—"

Before he could say more, she leaned forward and wrapped her lips around his erection.

"Paige!"

Both her hands gripped him tight, sliding up and down along the length of him while she sucked and swirled her tongue over his crown. His body was thrumming with energy, his shaft a live-wire sending out arcs of sensation along his nervous system. The *wanting* increased. More of this, more of her.

The coiled energy burst forth, exploding into her mouth as she kept pumping him. Shockwaves of an ecstasy more intense than anything he had ever experienced crashed through him, keeping time with the pulsing of his penis.

Echoing tremors of pleasure rippled out from where they touched as she let him slide from her mouth. He was finally softening again. All he could do was stare at her.

"Better?" she asked.

"I... Yes."

She stood, and said, "You might want to put that away."

He was buzzing with energy, his awareness of everything heightened as he stood as well. The scent of her body, the heat, the dampness left on his penis as he slid it into his jeans and fastened them again.

She wasn't smiling.

"Something is troubling you," he said.

"I'm fine. We should go."

She was radiating tension. His body felt more relaxed than ever. Relaxed and yet alert. Ready to defend her, to see to her needs. Perhaps that was the issue. If she had felt half of what he did, her body must be aching.

"I can...see to your needs," he said. The idea would have revolted him just a few hours ago. Now he was excited, eager to experience more with her. The attraction he had felt since they first met had intensified. He wanted to kiss her again.

"No thanks. Deflowering virgins is not my thing. Especially since I was the only one around to help out."

She said the last under her breath, but his hearing was too keen to miss it.

"You think what happened between us was purely based on circumstance."

"Wasn't it?" She crossed her arms and glared at him.

Stars, that glare. He had over a foot on her and at least a hundred pounds, and she looked as if she was planning to take his head off. With the right training, he had no doubt she could.

"Partly. Not purely."

She rolled her eyes. He smiled, which earned him a look even more heated than the first. Anger, yes. But passion. So much passion.

"I have never met anyone like you," he said.

"What—someone who's willing to blow you while you destroy their favorite chair?"

"Someone who is alive."

"Please don't tell me you're all space zombies. The vampire frogs are bad enough."

He laughed, and her expression softened the slightest bit. Her hair was dry, the coppery waves framing her face and making him want to touch her again. Why not allow himself?

He lifted the ends of her hair with just his fingertips,

letting the strands fall feather-light across his skin. She didn't seem to mind.

"Zombies, no. But sleepwalkers. All of us. You have no idea what it's like being created in the Coalition. Existing among septillions of others without ever connecting."

"Well, now that you know what you're missing, maybe you can find a nice Sadirian and—"

"I don't want someone else. Others have approached me. But no one else has ever…captivated me. Since the moment we met—"

"Stop. Don't get your hopes up and don't pin dreams onto me because of what happened between us. I don't do relationships."

He swallowed hard, sensing that this moment was pivotal for them both. He stepped closer.

"I told you that I'm considered a glitch."

"And I told you I don't like that word."

"You aren't supposed to. None of us are. It's used to remind us of our place, that we don't belong with successful results."

Her lips pressed into a thin line. Stars, he wanted to kiss her again. He let himself lift his hands to her arms, savoring the warmth and softness of her skin.

"Even among others like me, I'm considered an outlier. The geneticists studied me for years to determine why I'm so different. All I have ever done is try to be a normal Sadirian—to fit in. The majority of our society use

Coupling alone. I didn't use it at all because I've always thought that if I could somehow exemplify what it means to at least *act* like a perfect Sadirian then perhaps I would gain some acceptance."

He was admitting the fact as much to himself as her. Deep down, he had always known he was searching for something. A sense of belonging, of value and worth. He had been trying to obtain it by being the perfect soldier, the perfect citizen. He had never let himself think that there might be another way.

Until Paige.

She lifted her hand to his face, trailing her cool fingers along his cheek.

"I accept you."

Her words struck him in the center of his chest. His breath rushed out as he bowed his head, trying to regain some control.

No, *composure*. Control was…overrated.

She sighed, then said, "That doesn't mean—"

Before she could finish her sentence, he leaned in and kissed her.

Chapter Seven

The stiffness and hesitancy Paige had noticed the first time she and Khel kissed was gone. He pulled her against his chest, savoring her lips before sliding his tongue between them. His hands grasped her waist, then moved down to caress her ass. He lifted her, and she wrapped her legs around his waist as he pressed her back against her door.

He was hard again. She wasn't as eager to help him with it this time.

Well, okay, physically, she was ready to tear off their clothes and let him keeping working his magic with his hands and lips. He was kneading her ass, rocking his hips against her in just the right places.

It didn't matter that he'd been genetically engineered. When it came to sex, the man was a natural.

But the other things he'd said, about connecting and finding acceptance… That was too much. She didn't want him to form attachments to her and then be disappointed.

Most of the guys she hooked up with took it for what it was. A one-time thing. They both walked away a little more relaxed and a whole lot happier. The few times guys had become clingy, she had shut them down quickly and fairly easily. She was committed to her job. She had never met someone who could match her passion.

Or had she?

The thought was unwelcome, but she followed it through anyway. Khel was as driven as she was. His worldview was in a tailspin, though. He had been dedicating himself to a society that shunned him and used him. And she *would* have something to say to his leaders when they finally made it to that ship.

As focused as he had been on that objective, he still had been able to have an open and flexible mind. He was realizing the problems with his society, *and wanted to do the work to fix them.* That was heady.

If she tried to shut Khel out, she didn't think he'd go quietly like the others. He would fight for her. She could tell. And it thrilled her down to her toes. Someone who could handle her, match her passion *and* her stubbornness.

It was terrifying.

She had only ever dated weak-willed guys. She could never admit it to herself before, but it was true. Khel was iron to match her steel. Her match.

No. No way.

She kissed him harder, trying to block out her thoughts. It was the situation, the craziness of it all. This was a false sense of connection based on danger, lust, and adrenaline.

He matched her intensity, his tongue driving into her

mouth to meet each parry. She ground her clit against him through their jeans, imagining what it would be like to have that huge dick buried deep inside of her, pulsing as he came.

He let go of her ass with one hand and slid his fingers up under her shirt. The warmth and strength of his palm soaked into her skin as he massaged her breast. He ran his thumb over her nipple, exploring the tight bud as it peaked beneath his touch.

With a grunt, he leaned back from her, unwrapping her legs from his waist so that she was standing again. Had he finished already? How disappointing.

She was a little dazed as he undid her pants and tugged her jeans down to her knees. He knelt before her, pulling her panties down as well.

"Khel..."

He looked up at her, blue eyes blazing with lust or... something stronger. He leaned forward, pressing his lips against the curls between her legs. His tongue lapped at her, sending threads of pleasure streaming through her body.

Yeah, he was a natural.

She shifted her legs as far apart as she could to give him better access. He must have taken that as an invitation, because he worked his hand between her thighs, sliding two of his fingers deep into her. Her core gripped his fingers, heightening the friction as he slid them in and out, her body sparking with each pull and thrust.

Her legs felt weak and the room was spinning. She reached up and held onto the coat hook attached to her door to try to steady herself. She wasn't sure she would ever truly feel grounded again after this.

After *him*.

His fingers moved within her, his lips sucking, pulling on her clit. He had to have done this before. There was no way he could hit all the right spots, match his movement with her need. There was no way they could fit so perfectly together.

Her body had a different opinion.

The pleasure he stoked in her built to critical mass as he slid a third finger deep, drawing on her clit more strongly, pumping her mercilessly.

Explosions of stimuli radiated out from where he worked her, pleasure racking her body. She felt her core clench around him, wanting more, wanting all of him. She wanted him to take down his pants and plunge into her. She had never wanted someone so badly.

The ecstasy kept on as he didn't let up, the room blacking out around them. Finally, he slowed and pulled away, leaving her panting, her body pulsing...

She swallowed a few times before she could say, "Are the lights off, or is it just me?"

"It isn't just you."

He stood, pulling her panties and jeans up. She fumbled

with the fasteners, then reached for him in the pitch blackness.

"It's the Tau Ceti," he said.

Chapter Eight

Khel had never hated anyone before. He was fairly certain he was feeling hatred for the Tau Ceti. They had interrupted a beautiful moment between him and Paige. They were threatening her life.

For that, if nothing else, they would die.

"We have to warn Harry," she said.

Harry? The security guard. Her concern was admirable, but Khel didn't think the Tau Ceti would bother with the Earthling. They had undoubtedly taken out the cameras when they shut down the building's power and wouldn't see the guard as a threat.

The total silence was eerie. No ventilation, no somewhat familiar hum of machinery built into the structure maintaining the environment. He had noticed the alien stillness the moment the lights went out.

Darkness would aid the Tau Ceti. He needed to get Paige back outside into the sun. He picked up her bag and handed it to her, then grabbed her other hand and led her from her office. Dim light filtered in from windows on the exterior wall.

"What about Harry?"

"He'll be fine," Khel whispered. "They're only interested in you."

"How do they even know I'm here? I mean, wouldn't they think that you'd already taken me to your ship?"

That was a good point. The Tau Ceti soldier that attacked her at the gym most likely followed her there from her apartment. But Khel doubted it had followed them to her office. It made more sense that the Tau Ceti were making a move on her workplace, trying to destroy the data she had collected without realizing they were too late. Well, too late if Paige and Khel could make it back to the *Arbiter* with what they had learned.

"We need to get outside," he said. "Is there another route besides the elevator?"

"The stairs." She pulled on his hand, leading him in a different direction. "Please tell me you have a stunner or something you can use against these guys."

"I had to leave everything behind. Coalition technology would show up too easily on their scans."

"And you brainiacs haven't found a way to address that?"

"The Coalition doesn't *want* technology to be easily hidden. We've had peace for tens of thousands of years. We aren't used to citizens...rebelling."

"It looks to me like the Tau Ceti are taking advantage of that."

They reached the door to the stairwell. Khel opened it

and glanced into the small space. Emergency lighting cast a washed out blue glow over the steps, leaving thick shadows in corners and alcoves large enough for a Tau Ceti to hide.

"I don't like the thought of being trapped in the stairwell with vampire space frogs clinging to the ceiling," she said.

"Neither do I. But I see no other options."

"Well, let's give ourselves the best chance."

She reached toward a small box on the wall near the stairs. It read, *FIRE ALARM PULL DOWN*.

"This will make a huge noise and cause lights to flash all over the building."

Brilliant. She looked at him briefly, smirking when he smiled and nodded.

"I hope it's on the same circuit as the emergency lighting so it still works." She pulled the lever.

Blazingly bright lights began flashing, accompanied by an ear-splitting alarm. The Tau Ceti were certain to be disoriented by it for a few moments.

"We need to move quickly," he said.

She nodded and followed him into the stairwell, both keeping their footsteps as light and soundless as possible. They started out on the fifth floor and managed to make it down three levels before Khel heard stomping steps coming toward them.

Paige pulled on his hand, leading him through the exit

to that level. She closed the door behind them as quietly and quickly as possible, then opened a small cabinet set into the wall. It held a red canister with a nozzle at its top. She made some adjustments to it as they waited for the Tau Ceti to get farther away—or come closer.

The doorknob turned. Khel tried to get in front of her, but she darted under his arm, holding the canister up between them and the door. The device must be some sort of weapon.

When the door opened, she only waited a moment before attacking. She pulled the trigger and vapor and a fluffy white substance sprayed from the nozzle. He could feel the cold emanating from the chemicals. It was a perfect offense against the Tau Ceti.

The cyborg screamed and flailed its arms, the substance making the ground beneath its feet slippery. Khel didn't waste the opportunity. He grabbed the Tau Ceti's disintegrator.

Footsteps were already coming toward them from above. He aimed the weapon at the blinded enemy and pulled the trigger. Death was instant and painless. Its body vaporized in a quick yellow burst of energy.

"What the hell was that? Did you just *kill* that guy?" Paige shouted.

Two other Tau Ceti appeared on the stairs above them. Khel aimed and fired again, hitting one. The other managed to duck out of sight.

Khel grabbed the canister from Paige and flung it across the hall, angling it so that it would clatter down the stairs. Hopefully, the remaining Tau Ceti would think it was them and follow the sound.

He pushed Paige back out of the line of sight and let the door close. She looked like she was about to say something, so he did the first thing that came to mind. He pressed her up against the wall and kissed her.

Stars, she tasted good. He struggled to keep his attention on his environment, listening for the one Tau Ceti that was left. Only seconds passed before the cyborg took the bait, following the sound of the canister's descent. Khel waited another second before breaking off the kiss and opening the door, aiming the disintegrator at the Tau Ceti just as it raised its own weapon and fired.

Khel's shot hit the cyborg in the chest, vaporizing it. The Tau Ceti hit the wall to Khel's left. The wall protecting Paige.

Panic, stark and piercing, shot through Khel's mind making it impossible to breathe. He couldn't turn his head toward her. If the wall hadn't been enough to protect her... If he looked and she wasn't there...

He felt her hands on him, pushing as if she was trying to knock him over. His breath rushed from his chest and his innards settled somewhat. When he looked down at her, the fury on her features made him light-headed with relief.

"You *killed* them!"

He didn't understand her anger.

"They would have done the same and worse to you."

"Couldn't you have—"

"What? Taken them into custody? There were three of them and we were unarmed until you helped me secure a weapon."

Temporarily, anyway. He needed to set it to self-destruct as soon as they were out of the building. He couldn't bring himself to part with it before then, but the only thing easier for the Tau Ceti to track than Coalition technology would be their own equipment.

"They are feeding on your people," he said. "Remember that. They killed everyone who was on the plane with Senator Conroy just to eradicate one target. What do you think they'd do to get what they want from you?"

Her rage faded, but she continued to scowl at him. "I don't like loss of life. Any life."

"Sometimes it can't be avoided. We have to make the best choices we can."

"Fine. But we're warning Harry."

He sighed, but nodded.

They ran down the stairs, careful of the slickness left by the weapon she had used. He would need to ask her about that eventually. After she was safely in his ship.

True to her word, when they reached the front exit she

tracked down the security guard. He was standing in front of the building.

"Miss Sloan! I'm so glad you and your friend are okay," he said.

Odd that he would already care about Khel's safety. And yet, it was strangely comforting.

"The fire department should be here any second," Harry said. "You were the only ones inside."

"That's great, Harry." Paige put her hand on the man's arm. "I can't be here when they arrive, but I need you to call this in. Listen, this isn't—"

A deafening boom sounded, the shockwave striking Khel's body as the windows in the top three floors of the building exploded. He threw himself on Paige to shield her from the glass that rained down around them.

"Shit!" Paige yelled. She looked above as flames licked out of the empty spaces, hungry for more oxygen to burn.

"Are you all right?" Khel grabbed her arms and shook her to get her attention. "Assess yourself."

"I'm fine," she said. "Harry?"

The guard's eyes were wide, but he nodded.

"We have to leave," Khel said.

She nodded. "Harry, whatever you do, don't go back in the building."

"I'm not an idiot. It looks like a gas main blew. We should all get away from the building in case there are more explosions."

"That's wise," Khel said. He released one of Paige's arms but held the other tight, leading her in the opposite direction. The guard seemed too stunned by the event to notice.

"They blew up the building to destroy my notes. My group was only using one floor," she said. "We were in this building because the work we're doing is considered harmless. There's a community college that sometimes has weekend classes here. Businesses, a charity."

"The Tau Ceti don't care what sort of casualties they cause as long as they aren't found out. Your authorities will find that this looks like an accident."

Her pace increased. "We need to get to the *Arbiter* and let your people know what's going on."

Finally. He knew better than to speak his thought aloud. Instead, he nodded.

Chapter Nine

Paige shifted closer to Khel as they rode the bus toward his ship. They had used her phone so he could give her a general idea of where it was located and they could find the best route to get there. He reached over and held her hand. He had disposed of the disintegrator already, trying to make sure they weren't tracked.

She didn't want to think about what he had done with it. Or that she sort of wished they had kept it with them.

"I still don't get it," she said. "Why does the Coalition want their technology to be so traceable?"

"They don't want our technology to fall into the wrong hands. It could be reverse-engineered, or used to upset the balance of power on a planet not ready for that level of advancement. That's one of the reasons I wasn't allowed to bring anything out of my ship. If I were to have an accident or an Earthling managed to get their hands on my equipment somehow, it could have catastrophic results."

She snorted, a joke coming out reflexively. "I managed to get my hands on your equipment, and I'd say things went rather well."

His face turned pink. "I haven't had a chance to thank

you for that. I appreciate your help."

"Yeah, they all do." She looked away, not wanting to ask her next question, but being unable to stop herself. "Is that why you reciprocated? To balance out the scales?"

"Of course not." He squeezed her hand a little tighter. "I did it because…I wanted to share that with you."

"Curiosity."

"Intimacy. I told you, I could have explored…physical interactions many times. I chose to do so with you."

Lucky me.

She might have been his first, but she doubted she would be his last. The amount of passion he had shown wasn't something he could put a lid back on. Hell, he'd probably go back to his ship and start a new trend of sex without that drug.

The thought of her lovers going on to other partners had never bothered her before. She wasn't sure why it would do so now. It wasn't like she could leave Earth to be with Khel or he could stay. She wasn't even sure she wanted that. Right?

And they weren't even lovers yet. Not really.

Yet.

"How far to your ship?" She kept her face turned toward the window.

"Not very. It's attached to the bottom of one of your highways in a section of the city that is sparsely inhabited."

"It's on the underside of an overpass in a crappy section of town. Fun." At least it was the middle of the day.

Had she really only met Khel a couple of hours ago? It seemed like so much longer. Being attacked by space frogs, having some pretty serious foreplay, and watching a building basically blow up made the time seem to dilate. That and the three people he had killed.

One had almost killed her. She would never forget seeing the wall in front of her just disappear, the Tau Ceti pointing his ray gun at her. Either he had been panicking or capturing her alive wasn't that important after all. Neither thought was reassuring.

They had killed Senator Conroy and everyone else on the plane with him. She would have died then, if it hadn't been for her micro-managing nature that kept her out in the field making sure the cleanup crew had accomplished their goals. There were always more samples to study, like the ones she had thought were off—contaminated somehow. Now she knew they weren't. The Tau Ceti were destroying Earth's ecosystems and *feeding* on humans.

She still couldn't wrap herself around the notion of killing them, though.

"When you tell your people what's going on here, are they going to kill all the Tau Ceti involved?" she asked.

"Only if necessary. The objective will be to take them into custody and send them through our tribunal process."

"That's nice I guess. How will you apprehend them?"

"Sorca, the head of security on the *Arbiter*, will come down with several teams on interceptors. They'll be armed with stunners. Her people will only use lethal force if necessary to defend themselves and others."

Paige let out a little breath of relief. "Do you have any of those 'stunners' on your ship?"

"I have two, plus a phase rifle. I was sent in a skimmer. It's a small ship with only the most basic levels of technology possible, designed for quick expeditions. I was supposed to pick you up and take you to the *Arbiter* before the Tau Ceti knew I was planetside."

"Guess I screwed that up."

"Our detour provided us with invaluable information."

"Only if we live long enough to share it."

He gently touched her cheek, turning her to face him. "We're going to make it, Paige. I won't let anything happen to you."

Then he leaned forward and kissed her again.

Heat welled up deep within her instantly. He left his hand on her cheek, his thumb lightly dusting her skin. She opened her mouth to him as his tongue slid inside, stroking her, savoring her, exploring the sensations.

She shifted closer to let as much of their bodies press together as she could manage. His free arm held her tight. She wanted to crawl into his lap and straddle him, but that would call more attention to them than was wise. At least, while they were on the bus. Once they reached his ship, everything was fair game.

"Hey, kissyfaces back there. Didn't you say you need me to stop at Third Avenue and Grand? That's coming up, and I ain't sticking around longer than it takes you to jump off the bus."

They broke off the kiss, both glaring at the driver. He glanced at them in the mirror and shook his head. A few other passengers were looking their way, grinning or scowling. Paige might have said something if the circumstances were different. As they were, she let it slide.

The bus pulled to the curb and she and Khel quickly made their way to the exit. She really hoped they had the location right. Even with his intimidating presence, she didn't want to be walking around in this neighborhood for long.

"This way." He interlaced their fingers and headed down the littered sidewalk.

His ship wasn't far, and the few people they encountered seemed put off enough by Khel's bulk to leave them alone. He led her through a torn up chain link fence toward the cement pillars that held up an overpass. Traffic whizzed by above them.

"The cloak will disengage automatically when we're close enough," he said. "I couldn't leave the ship on the ground without running the risk of someone bumping into it within the city."

"How are we going to get into it?"

He smiled down at her and her heart sort of skipped a bit.

How embarrassing.

"You'll see."

He stopped, his smile deepening. Then he looked up. She followed his gaze and gasped.

"Oh, wow."

A black ship with a crescent moon shape hung above them, clinging to the highway like a bat. It had curved wings that arced up away from them.

Though she never let herself own a car, she did indulge in admiring them. She'd always had a particularly soft spot for shiny muscle cars with sleek lines. This vehicle was even better—a masterpiece. Its lines sang like a symphony, entrancing her gaze. A hatch opened near the center of its mass, and a ladder slowly descended toward them.

"Okay, I'm pretty sure I would do you just for your ride. Wait, that didn't come out right."

Khel grinned as he guided her onto the ladder. He climbed on behind her, wrapping his arms around her and caging her against its metal rungs, presumably to keep her safe. Then again, as his hips pressed against her ass, she wondered.

The ladder began to rise. Her heart was beating fast. Heights weren't her thing. Even scarier, she realized she felt safe in Khel's arms.

And worst of all—she was starting to get used to it.

Chapter Ten

Finally, they were safely on his ship. Khel felt himself relax a bit more. He would breathe easier yet once they were on the *Arbiter*. Even though the hatch had closed, he held Paige tight against the ladder as he initiated the ship's basic systems.

"Ship, reengage cloak." He paused, listening for the familiar buzz that let him know the cloak was back in place. Now for the tricky part. "Engage artificial gravity field—level zero only."

Slowly, weightlessness settled over them. Paige was still clinging to the ladder that had folded itself into the airlock wall as it lifted them into the ship. She looked over her shoulder at him, her eyes wide. Her hair floated around her face.

He used his training to keep them in place, but couldn't help but notice how her body drifted against his. Zero-G had always been an environment to be processed and adapted to. Experiencing it with Paige made it seem like an opportunity. He imagined the two of them in deep space together, turning off the gravity field and seeing what they could accomplish.

"Lean into me," he said. "You can trust me."

Her lips pressed tight again, but she relaxed a little. She had seemed afraid while the ladder ascended. Perhaps exploring Zero-G maneuvers with her would need to wait.

He wrapped one leg around hers and lifted them both from what was normally the top of the airlock's cabin. Arcing his back while keeping her pressed against him, he brought their feet to the floor 'above'.

Relative to Earth's gravity field, they were upside-down —not that it mattered with his ship blocking that out. He twisted around using the ladder so they would be standing upright when the ship's gravity kicked in, then gave the command.

"Initiate standard gravity field."

He had never been more aware of the pull of the ship's gravity on his body. He watched as Paige's hair descended around her shoulders.

Stars, he wanted to kiss her. But she still looked distressed.

"Are you all right?" he asked.

"I'm a little stunned, I guess. Are we upside-down?"

"Only relative to Earth's gravity."

"This is so weird." She glanced around the small airlock. "I'm on an actual spaceship. In an artificial gravity field."

"Let me show you the rest of the ship."

Especially the sleeping chamber. It was located just on

the other side of the airlock wall, but there wasn't direct access. Instead, they would need to descend into the main cabin of the ship, then climb another ladder to reach it.

He placed his palm on the panel that would open the hatch to the rest of the ship. Hand and footholds were set into the wall below.

"Let me go first," he said.

He barely fit through the hatch and always found the holding spots too closely spaced. When he reached the floor, he could still touch her if he stretched. Skimmers were not designed with Khel's dimensions in mind. They were meant to be snug even for normal Sadirians, both for efficiency and safety. If the gravity field malfunctioned, they wouldn't have far to fall.

Paige stared down at him for a few moments before cautiously sitting next to the hatch and swinging her legs over the edge. She passed him her bag, which he set on the floor.

"You'll catch me, right?"

"Of course."

"I just...don't like heights. And it is seriously messing with me thinking that I would actually be falling up toward outer space."

"Then don't think about it. Come to me."

She smirked, but slid over the edge, not even bothering with the wall. He caught her easily enough.

"That was amazing," she said.

Every new experience they had shared amazed him. Even simply standing as he was, holding her with her arms wrapped around his neck, knowing that he could kiss her, touch her, and it would feel…natural.

He lowered her to the floor so she could look around. Following her, he tried to imagine his ship from her perspective.

The main cabin of the skimmer was like all Coalition ships. The design was minimalistic, with controls built into the walls identifiable only by etchings in the otherwise smooth metal. Once activated, readouts and command options would illuminate on the displays.

Grooves in the walls at various stations acted as hand-holds and places to connect safety straps that extended from their uniforms in the case of sudden gravity loss. He should probably change back into his uniform, but found Earth clothes to be quite comfortable. Plus he already associated them with extremely positive experiences.

"Is there a way we can see outside?" she asked.

He walked to the appropriate controls and opened the screens that covered the ship's viewports. He wondered what she thought of seeing the world upside-down. As he hoped, she smiled as she approached.

"That is trippy. It really feels like we're the ones who are right-side up."

"Space travel is one of the most important cornerstones of the Coalition. Addressing the issue of artificial gravity was a necessary early step in the development of our society. It was worked out millennia ago."

"Before things became peaceful and you guys stopped inventing things."

He didn't have a response to that. He couldn't deny that the Coalition hadn't been making many technological advancements lately. Like in the last few centuries. Even genetic engineering advancements were simply fine-tuning the process to perfect the desired results and minimize glitches like him.

"So you can cloak your ships but not your weapons," she said.

"Portable tech is too small to contain cloaking generators. Otherwise it wouldn't be an issue."

"I still think the Coalition should work on that. At least blocking scans, even if the stuff isn't completely cloaked. Maybe build in a self-destruct sequence if you don't key in a unique identifier within a specified timeframe or something."

That could actually work, if any of the decision-makers still cared enough to try to improve procedures. "I'll relay your suggestion as soon as we get to the *Arbiter*."

"I guess we'll be heading out soon, then?"

"Actually, we need to wait until nightfall. There's always a chance that the cloak will fail. Protocol dictates that arrivals and departures in urban areas of non-Coalition planets happen at night. That's also why skimmers have dark hulls."

"Can we at least send them a message with what we discovered?"

"I think we should wait." He could have insisted, but knew she would appreciate being part of the decision. He *wanted* her to be part of the decision. "The first Tau Ceti that attacked us escaped. It's undoubtedly informed its superiors that I'm in the area. Since the three that attacked your office building didn't return, they must know we haven't left yet. They'll be scanning for us actively. We should send the transmission right before we leave."

"I guess that makes sense. It won't be dark for hours, though." She smiled up at him. "What would you like to do to fill the time?"

He smiled back, putting his hands on her waist and pulling her closer. "There's one more section of the ship you haven't seen yet. The sleeping chamber."

She wrapped her arms around his neck. "I'm not tired."

"I am very glad to hear that."

He bent down to kiss her, memorizing the softness of her lips, the velvet feel of her tongue. Slowly, he walked them back to the recesses that acted as hand and footholds set into the wall that led to the sleeping chamber. He lightened his kiss and reached out to press his hand against the access panel for the hatch above. She pulled away as it slid open, glancing up.

"I'll be right behind you," he said.

She nodded, then turned and started up the wall. He helped her find the places to put her hands and feet, letting his grip linger on her backside as she climbed. When she reached the top, she disappeared over the edge. He followed her quickly.

The sleeping chamber was even more cramped than the main cabin. Khel bent over a bit to avoid hitting his head on the ceiling. Paige had no trouble standing upright in the small space.

"Cozy," she said. She angled her head toward the regen bed. "Do you even fit in that?"

"Barely." He was using Adam's skimmer, which had a specially crafted regen bed that was larger than most. Adam was a few inches shorter than Khel, but the bed had been made with extra room for his comfort. Khel's toes touched one end while his hair brushed the other.

"The floor looks pretty comfortable," she said. "And it's a lot more spacious."

"I sometimes use it for rest." He rolled out the mat he had brought along for that purpose.

"Nice."

She pulled her shirt over her head and tossed it on the floor. Khel lowered himself to his knees to better watch her. She smiled as she kicked off her shoes and reached down to pull off her socks. Then she undid her jeans and slowly slid them down her legs. She stepped out of them and tossed them away.

The undergarments she wore were a matching pale blue. He hadn't really noticed that before. He had seen stars a similar shade. The fabric looked soft, with intricate designs woven into it. He wondered what it would feel like against his skin.

"I'm getting way ahead of you, Khel. Might want to catch up."

He drew his shirt over his head and cast it aside, then shifted to sit so he could take off his boots and socks. Undressing in front of her, he felt oddly vulnerable. She had been graceful in her movements, making it a sensual dance. He couldn't even stand up in the room.

"Hold on a moment," she said. "Could you kneel for me again?"

He happily did as she asked.

"We have plenty of time," she said. "I want us to enjoy ourselves."

She knelt in front of him, then placed her hands on his hips and guided him to rise up on his knees. Then she undid his jeans for him, as she had before. This time, her soft smile alluded to pleasures he could barely imagine. He was trying, though.

He thought of resting above her, his penis buried deep in her warm, pulsing core. Or with her on top, her breasts rubbing against his chest as she moved on him. He was glad he had forced himself to study the logistics of sex, even though he had never planned to use *Coupling*.

He still never planned to use it.

She reached into his jeans, gently running her fingertips over his rigid shaft. Arcs of pleasure ran through his body. She continued the feather-light touches for a few more moments before wrapping her fingers around him and gently moving her hand up and down.

"Paige," he moaned.

"Yes?" She increased the pressure of her grip. His eyes rolled shut.

"*Coupling*—"

Her hand stopped moving on him, but she didn't let him go. "I have no interest in trying out your space sex drug."

His eyes snapped open and he laughed. "That isn't what I was about to suggest."

"Oh. Well, good." She started moving her hand again and he groaned.

"*Coupling* prevents pregnancy. My people are still fertile, even though we're genetically engineered."

"We don't have to worry about that. I have an IUD. It prevents pregnancy."

"Excellent." The word came out like a purr and she laughed.

"And we already covered the whole disease thing," she said. "I know you said you're inoculated against Earth stuff, but I do get tested regularly and have always used condoms before."

"What's a condom?"

She laughed. "Some day I'll show you one. Might be fun to change things up."

She paused again, her brow furrowing for the briefest of moments.

"What is it?"

"Nothing." She shook her head and smiled, but it seemed a bit forced. "I want to focus on this moment. Let's not think of anything else. Just you and me and right now. Deal?"

No thoughts of duty or the Tau Ceti or the *Arbiter* awaiting them. Only Paige, and her cool touch and warm heart. Her passion.

He could do that.

"Agreed."

"Excellent." She grinned as she mimicked his statement from earlier. Then she bent her head to him and drew him into her mouth.

So much pleasure. Warmth and wetness cascading along his nerve endings as she swirled her tongue around his crown and flicked it over the length of his shaft.

He wanted to touch her. He buried his fingers in her hair, gently encouraging her, trying to keep himself from plummeting over the edge into the ecstasy she promised. He felt himself getting too close, and just before he said something, she stopped.

"Lay back for me," she said.

Unable to form words, he simply obeyed. How could

she read his body so well? She pulled his jeans from his legs, then reached behind her back to unclasp her bra. Rising, she slid off her panties, then stood with one leg on either side of him.

Was she contemplating falling on top of him and letting him plunge into her immediately? His penis jerked at the thought. But he wanted to give her the same pleasure she had been giving him.

He sat up, which brought him perfectly in range to reciprocate. Her legs were long enough the he only had to arch his back a bit to press a kiss to the softest folds of her flesh.

He brought his hands first to her buttocks, kneading her flesh and tracing their curves. She moaned as he pressed deeper with his tongue, flicking her clitoris as she had done to his shaft.

Resting one arm behind her to help stabilize her, he used his free hand to delve into her with first one, then two fingers. Her body took him in eagerly. He added a third, and she gasped, stiffening and pulling away.

"Too soon," she said. "I want the next one to be together."

He nodded, though he had no idea how to achieve that objective.

"Tell me what to do."

She put her hands on his shoulders, pushing him to the floor and joining him, knees on either side of his hips. She kissed him with a tenderness and passion that left him breathless. Then she shifted her kisses along his chin and jaw, making her way to his neck just below his ear. Goosebumps rippled across the surface of his body. Her voice was a breathy whisper.

"We just need to listen to our bodies and share what we're experiencing, especially when we're getting closer to the edge." She nuzzled his ear. "It's like electricity humming just above your skin, leaving you wondering when the lighting will strike."

Chapter Eleven

That lightning was already gathering in Paige's body. Khel had almost sent her over the edge with his unexpected and amazing foreplay. She was glad he seemed as worked up as she was. But she wanted to make sure they were in synch.

She lowered her hips to his, pressing his shaft into her slit. Sliding over his length, she brought herself back toward that edge, letting her body wet him and help them both be ready for him to enter her. His dick was huge, and she wanted to enjoy every second of him without a moment of discomfort.

His breath was hitching and his eyes were closed, his fingers clasping her ass and squeezing as she moved. Yeah, they were probably both ready. Still, she hesitated.

She had never let a man into her body without a condom before. Beyond knowing that there was minimal risk of physical consequences, the intimacy they were about to share was something she had never allowed herself with anyone.

Khel isn't just anyone.

She pushed the thought out of her head. They weren't

supposed to be thinking—just experiencing. Focusing on each other and the pleasure they were sharing. Everything else could wait.

With one last long glide along his shaft, she lined up his crown and began slowly inching down over him. He was thick, spreading her flesh, making her feel tight. She let out a slow breath, willing her body to relax, to expand to welcome him. She had to back off a few times, sliding him most of the way out before easing him back in. Finally, she sat back, taking him in fully, his dick filling her.

She didn't dare move. If she did, she would go off. Judging by the look on his face, he was in the same boat. His eyebrows had drawn together so tight, they were forming a single line across his forehead. The idea almost made her giggle, which was good. It helped her to cool off, to gain some distance.

"Take a deep breath and let it out slowly," she said.

He complied without opening his eyes. The wrinkles between his eyebrows lessened infinitesimally.

"Good," she said. "Now talk to me. Tell me what you're feeling."

He shook his head.

"It might help you last longer."

He swallowed hard. "I don't want…this to end. Ever."

She smiled, then slowly inched up along his shaft. The friction was setting off spirals of pleasure that echoed through her, resonating along her skin.

"We can always do it again." She slid back down, taking him all the way in. "And again, and again."

He finally opened his eyes. So much passion. Such intensity.

It scared her.

"Not the sex," he said. "You. Being with you. I don't want—"

She kissed him before he could say anything else. Her heart was hammering in her chest.

She didn't do commitment. She wasn't that girl. She answered her body's needs, had the occasional fun romp, and always—*always*—walked away.

But with Khel…she didn't want to.

These thoughts were unwelcome. She shifted her focus to her body, to the ecstatic feeling of his dick filling her, pulling against her flesh. She tightened the muscles of her core, milking him, pushing him closer to the edge as she increased her pace.

Sitting back, she felt him rock into her, his hips pumping, grip tightening. The sensations were swirling around where they connected—*were* connected. Physically. Just physically.

Electricity scattered across her nerves, building until the lightning struck, branching through her body, filling every cell until she felt herself radiating energy. He cried out, his back arcing and his hips bucking against hers, pounding his dick into her as he came. She felt every pulse, her body echoing it, pulling on it, wanting more.

She wanted…more. More than this fleeting pleasure. More than a one-night stand.

His eyes were wide as he stared at her. Dammit, he was feeling it, too.

It had to be an illusion. The adrenaline of the situation, being thrown together. Feelings this intense didn't happen so quickly. Not real feelings.

This wasn't love.

"That was…" he said. "I've never…"

"That makes two of us." She smiled as she let him slide from her body, feeling grateful for the distance and missing the connection at the same time. She wanted to run away, screaming. Instead, she made herself lie next to him and tried to relax.

"Listen, you should know that sex can make you feel an artificial sense of connection," she said.

"You feel it, too," he said.

Oh crap.

"I feel… It doesn't matter. Stressful situations can make people feel closer. And adding sex to that can make it worse."

"You're trying to dismiss what I feel—what *we* feel. Calling it 'artificial'. Nothing about this is artificial. Are you truly going to tell me to ignore my emotions after everything you've said? Everything we've done? Did it only apply to *physical* feelings?"

Honestly, that's what she had been focusing on. But damn Khel with his drive and his passion and his amazing body. He was the total package. She just wasn't looking to buy.

"It doesn't matter," she said again. "You guys don't even have real sex. I highly doubt you have partners or marriage or—"

"We pair-bond. My people still decide to partner with others. It can be a mutually beneficial arrangement, or because of mutual attraction. We still fall in love."

She rolled away from him and sat up. "But not in half a day. Nobody falls in love that fast."

"From what I understand, falling in love is a process. Who is to say how it begins or will proceed?"

He sat up next to her, but didn't reach for her. She wanted him to, and cursed herself for it. Of all the people to fall for—or start to fall for, as he pointed out—an alien?

"This isn't a passing thing for me," he said. "I am forever changed. Not from the coupling or the threat of the Tau Ceti. Because of you."

And that was the problem. He had changed her, too.

Chapter Twelve

Pair-bonding had always seemed an archaic and unnecessary social construct. Now, Khel was wondering what would be involved in formalizing a relationship with Paige.

He didn't really care about paperwork. He just wanted to be with her. From everything she'd said and done, it didn't seem one-sided. Then again, he was new to this.

Paige grabbed her undergarments and pulled them up her legs, then started shimmying into her jeans. "Infatuation isn't love. Admittedly, the sex has been great, but we'll get over it in a couple of..." She paused and glanced at him. "Months."

She didn't look convinced, which encouraged him. He stood, hunched over, but didn't bother with his clothes. She dug through the pile and pulled out her bra, struggling with the straps in her haste.

As she sorted her clothing out, she repeated, "We'll get over it."

Khel was silent as she dressed. He waited until she'd pulled her shirt back over her head to speak.

"Do you want to?" he asked.

"Want to what?"

"Get over me."

Her mouth dropped open and she paused in the middle of pulling on her shoe. Before she had a chance to answer, the gravity field failed. There was no shift through Zero-G. Up was suddenly down.

Khel was inches away from the ceiling. He felt the first tug of Earth's gravity and launched himself at Paige, trying to catch her before her head struck the hull. He barely made it in time, curling himself around her and altering her trajectory so that she wouldn't injure her head, neck, or spine. They ended up in a pile on the ceiling, his sleeping mat and clothes strewn over them.

"What the hell was that?" she asked.

"I don't know. Ship, report." Nothing. "Ship—"

The light in the chamber was coming from the small viewport in the sleeping chamber. He had left the screens open after Paige requested a view.

No power. That meant no defenses and no cloak. At least they were still firmly attached to the highway overhead.

A rending sound tore away that small comfort. The hull groaned, and the screech of metals grinding together rang in his ears as something attached to the ship and pulled. He scrambled to the viewport. Paige hurried after.

A large transport with an Earth-style exterior was parked right beneath them. It looked like a large semi truck, but the top of the trailer was open, revealing technology the likes of which Khel had never seen. Part of it included a grappling arm that had attached to the skimmer. There were two other arms with some sort of sonic cutters at the ends, the beams slicing through the wings of his ship.

"Khel…"

He didn't have time to reassure her. The force of the grappling arm attached to his ship had to be impacting the highway overhead. If the stress grew too great, it would pull the busy pathway apart, endangering scores of Earthlings.

He pushed Paige toward the hatch that led below. She grabbed his clothing as they went. Lifting her, she crawled up into the ship's main cabin area. She had to be filled with questions, with fear. But she was trusting him and following his lead. The thought fortified him for what was to come.

He lifted himself through the hatch, then ran to the manual release for the docking clamps. He pried off the cover for the lever and pulled on it with all his strength. With any luck, the skimmer would be too heavy for the grappling claw and would crush the Tau Ceti beneath them.

He felt the clamps start to give and shouted, "Brace yourself!"

Instead of the sudden drop he had hoped for, the ship

only shuddered. He heard a rending sound—most likely the wings coming off. Metal scraped metal as the remains of his skimmer descended. They stabilized at a slight angle, no doubt so the ship would fit into the vehicle. Through the viewport, they could see the light slowly vanish as the top of the trailer closed.

No power. No cloak. No weapons, propulsion, shields...or communication. How had the Tau Ceti managed to disable his ship? How had they found him in the first place? And most importantly, how was he going to protect Paige?

A light appeared in the inky darkness. Paige's phone.

"You said we'd be safe when we reached your ship," she said. There was no accusation in her tone. Her voice was flat and calm.

"I thought we would be. I'm so sorry."

"Save the apologies. Right now, we need a plan."

He wouldn't let either of them fall into Tau Ceti hands. The only plan he could think of involved a well-placed phase rifle set to overload and a final kiss—if he could even get his weapons to work. The ship had been thoroughly neutralized.

"Your silence is not encouraging."

"This is unprecedented," he said. "The Tau Ceti have disabled my ship. Without power, there's nothing I can do to protect us."

"I'm not going down without a fight. Where do you

keep your weapons?"

He led her to the panel for the weapons' locker and opened it. Everything on the ship was meant to control enemies, not kill them. He grabbed a stunner and tried to power it up. Nothing.

"Okay, then." She turned her phone toward her face, working on the screen. "I'm not getting a signal, so they're probably blocking me. But I still have power. Why would that be?"

"They must only be targeting Coalition technology. The ship's hull blocks transmissions. It's part of the design. Only the communications array built into the ship will relay messages."

"And the Tau Ceti have shut that down. Which is good for us."

"What?"

She glanced toward him, grinning. "They think they have us beat because they've taken out your ship. But they've underestimated our Earth technology."

"They know about phones. I doubt we'll make it off the ship without them commandeering it."

"But will they bother trying to block its signal? Will they even be watching for one from me?"

"I don't know."

"Would you?"

He thought for a moment, then shook his head. "No. Earth technology is rudimentary. There aren't any signals worth blocking. Taking your phone would be enough for me. Besides, anyone on the planet you could try to call for assistance would be completely outgunned."

"*Anyone on the planet.*" She started using the light from her phone to look around his ship. "But if I can get a signal to orbit—"

He shook his head. "Your cell phone won't be able to reach Brendan, if that's what you're thinking. And, as I said, they'll most likely commandeer it immediately."

The light from her phone crossed her backpack. She quickly ran to it. "That's not what I'm thinking."

She dug around in her bag, then pulled out a small plastic cylinder. It looked completely unremarkable.

"What is that?"

"A panic button. It's made to look like lipstick. The signal it emits is supposed to be untraceable."

"There is no Earth technology that is untraceable."

"Yeah, and the Tau Ceti can't see through your cloaks, either. If this can send a signal even for a few moments, Brendan might be able to pick up on it."

He knew she was grasping for hope. Hope he tried to share.

"You might be ready to give up, but I'm not," she said. "This is our best shot. I'm going to take it."

He wished she was half as interested in keeping their relationship alive. If so, they would stand a chance. He was further aggravated that her zeal only made her that much more attractive.

Shaking aside his thoughts, he set his priorities straight. First, fight the Tau Ceti...after getting dressed. And if they survived, he would fight for a chance with Paige.

Chapter Thirteen

"There has to be something around here we can use as a weapon." Paige was racking her brain, trying to come up with anything else that might give them an edge.

She was the first to admit—if only to herself—that the panic button was a longshot. Though she suspected Brendan had it hooked up to satellites, she couldn't be sure. He had always denied it when she asked.

Even if it could reach Brendan, the Tau Ceti might scan her and find the signal. They might have a general jamming device wherever they were taking her and Khel.

Then again, they might not. If she'd learned anything about these aliens, it's that they were cocky bastards. The Coalition had been coasting for so long, it sounded like they were falling to entropy. And the Tau Ceti thought of Earthlings as walking snacks, not cunning adversaries.

Even if the Tau Ceti took away her bag, the panic button would keep emitting its signal. Brendan would eventually find it—find her. She only hoped it would be in time.

She shook aside the dark thought. They were going to get through this. And afterwards…

Afterwards, she'd have to give Khel his answer. As much as she would prefer not to.

She *didn't* want to get over him.

The thought of following this new relationship through to its natural conclusion scared her more than facing the Tau Ceti. When she let herself think of where she and Khel were headed, she actually imagined them as weathered from time. Did his people age the same way as Earthlings? She had never considered growing old with someone before. She shelved that question for later.

"Maybe we can use the rifle as a club," she said. Or chuck the ray guns at the Tau Ceti.

She shook her head at her own ridiculous thought, but then another popped in. A possibly viable one.

"You said your tech is programmed to self-destruct. Is there any way we can bring that system back online? And if we did, would it be powerful enough to take them out or cause a diversion?"

"It would be, but they'll be on guard for that. Kira used the self-destruct sequence for the listening station where she was assigned to observe Earth. She took out a fair number of the Tau Ceti when she did so, along with one of their ships."

"Remind me to thank her, whoever she is."

"Your brother's partner."

"Partner?"

"Yes. She broke protocol and began conversing with

him several months ago. Apparently, they fell in love. They've gone so far as to enter their pair-bond into Coalition records."

What the hell? Her ears started to buzz.

Everything going on around her, and this caused her to freak out. "Brendan got married and didn't tell me? I'm going to kill him!"

"There were and continue to be exigent circumstances."

"Still... The guy is at the forefront of communication technology on Earth. He could have called."

"It's been less than a day."

Right. Everything was happening at light speed. She leaned against the wall, closing her eyes for a moment and taking deep breaths to try to center herself. Khel's soft touch on her cheek didn't startle her. She had felt his warmth as he approached.

"I can't promise you that everything will be okay," he said. "But I will die protecting you."

She let out a brief laugh. "I don't want you to die. I want both of us to live. So cut it out with that kind of talk. I'm just trying to find some balance here."

"Balance?"

"Emotional equilibrium. Or don't you super-advanced aliens need to worry about that anymore?"

In the dim light from her phone, she could see him thinking.

"The Coalition provides a chemical for that. It's even

called *Balance*."

"That's the first thing you've told me about the Coalition that reassures me. I'm glad they're using their advancements to help people with imbalances in their brain chemistry."

"There are no imbalances in brain chemistry. The regen beds take care of that. *Balance* is for all citizens, to keep them content and maintain peace."

"You've got to be kidding me. They're prescribing happiness? Does the Coalition allow its citizens to experience *anything* that's real?"

His silence said more than any words could. She was getting close to the limits of what she could take. Vampire space frogs were bad enough. But the more she learned about the Coalition, the more turning to them for help seemed like an, 'out of the frying pan' situation.

"Brendan and Kira weaponized *Balance* against the Tau Ceti," Khel said.

Now he had her interest. "How?"

"Sadirians apply it topically. The Tau Ceti have sensitive skin. *Balance* helps Sadirians feel well adjusted. For the Tau Ceti, it makes them euphoric and then knocks them out."

"What are you suggesting?" she asked. "That we palm some and try to shake everyone's hands?"

"There isn't much on board. But if we use it at the right moment, we might be able to escape."

They didn't even know where they were being taken. For all they knew, the Tau Ceti were just moving Khel's ship to a less conspicuous spot before vaporizing it and everyone on board. Except the Tau Ceti still wanted to know what she knew. From what Khel had said, she had a feeling vaporization would be preferable to their questioning techniques. She hoped to avoid both scenarios.

"I have specimen containers in my bag," she said. "If we transfer this chemical into them, the Tau Ceti will be less likely to take it away."

"Brilliant."

They worked together to get it done. They were just finishing when she felt the truck carrying the ship slow to a stop. She reached into her bag and hit the panic button, then buried it at the bottom, keeping the specimen containers full of *Balance* near the top.

Khel quickly hid the empty *Balance* vials in one of the panels in the ship's walls while she slid her backpack's strap over her shoulder. He came to stand at her side, finding her hand and interlacing their fingers.

The ship lurched, and they grabbed onto each other more tightly. Light filtered into the ship as the top of the vehicle carrying them opened. She could see trees covered in sphagnum moss through the viewport and prayed the Tau Ceti weren't planning on dumping them in the swamp to drown or starve.

The ship began to turn. The ceiling they were standing

on became a ramp as they slowly spun back to an upright position. Khel held her waist, helping them slide safely to the wall and then land on the floor when the ship settled.

More sunlight illuminated the ship as a ramp in the flooring opened. Two Tau Ceti cyborgs marched aboard. She was beginning to recognize the clunking sound of their steps. Advanced technology, yet they hadn't bothered to try to make them light on their feet. It was just another symptom of how individuals seemed to be devalued in both cultures.

A man wearing a white hat and suit walked up the ramp. His bow tie was a thin black ribbon. His eyes were large and protruded from his head in a very frog-like way. His lips were thick and his face gaunt.

"Good evening," he said, in a thick Southern accent.

Okay. She wasn't expecting that.

For some reason, it made him even creepier. He was an alien. He was supposed to sound alien, not like one of the locals.

"My apologies for the accommodations during your trip. I'm afraid there's one further formality before we can move forward."

He gestured to one of the cyborgs. Paige put up a little resistance—mostly for show—as they took her phone. The guy patted her down, then Khel. He handed Paige's phone to the guy in the white suit.

"Thank you for leaving the screen unlocked," he said.

After messing with it for a moment, he put it in his pocket. "Your battery's looking a bit low."

"It's not meant to be used to light up a spaceship," she said.

"Again, my apologies. Let's head outside and enjoy some fresh air and refreshments."

Was he kidding? He bowed slightly and turned, walking down the ramp. His two goons stepped forward menacingly. Yeah, he wasn't kidding. Khel took her hand and walked next to her as they left his ship.

The heat and humidity struck her senses. She looked around, trying to figure out where they were. All she saw was swamp. She remembered the maps they had focused on at her office. This could easily be one of those locations.

The guy—space frog—in the white suit led them along a narrow trail that opened up onto an immense and immaculate lawn. A huge mansion sat fifty yards away. He led them to a gazebo instead.

Trees towered above, casting the spot in perpetual shade. The space frog trotted up the stairs and sat at one of four chairs around a circular table, then gestured for them to join him.

She cast a glance at Khel as they followed. When he nodded, they both sat. Someone she presumed was another Tau Ceti brought a tray of what looked like lemonade and small sandwiches.

The Tau Ceti who had greeted them on the ship took off his white hat and set it on the table. "I'm Norm. Would you care for something to eat or drink?"

"No thanks," Paige said.

"Whatever makes you happy."

She snorted. "What, so we'll make a tastier snack later?"

Norm smiled, then took a sip of lemonade. "I've read all about you, Paige Elizabeth Sloan. Crusaders have a bitter finish. Too much adrenaline."

"What can I say? I love my job—and my planet."

"We have that in common. Well, the part about loving the planet. Earth is amazing. It's become a very popular retreat."

"Yeah. I see you Tau Ceti guys are really making yourselves at home."

Norm laughed. "You must expand your thinking, Ms. Sloan. It's true that we've carved out a little territory for our own recreational activities. But the Coalition's umbrella falls over hundreds of thousands of sentient species, each with their own environmental needs—not that the Sadirians really stop to think about that often."

He cast a brief glare at Khel before resuming his friendly expression. "Earth is truly one of the most amazing planets we've encountered. Such varied ecosystems. It's capable of supporting so many different forms of life."

Paige's stomach knotted. She thought they were only dealing with the Tau Ceti. What he was alluding to was much worse.

"You know, this doesn't have to end badly for you," he said. "Your expertise could be quite beneficial for myself and my colleagues."

"Set up your own damn spawning pools," she said.

His eyebrows hitched up his forehead and he smiled. "See? That's exactly what I mean. Even the planetary liaison we've been working with hadn't figured out what we were up to. Mostly because he didn't care. But you care, Ms. Sloan."

He leaned forward and closed his eyes, inhaling deeply through his nose. When he sat back and opened his eyes, his gaze was predatory. "It's written all over your scent."

She lurched forward, grabbing the pitcher of lemonade and getting ready to club him with it. Khel grabbed her arm and held her still. She looked past Norm to the two armed cyborg guards who had leveled weapons at her.

Norm was just smiling. He gestured to the guards to stand down and they did. Khel gently guided her hand to set the pitcher down, then they both eased back into their seats. He squeezed her wrist lightly before letting her go.

"Earthlings," Norm said. "So passionate. So many delicious emotions. I myself have been cultivating a taste for any number of the chemicals associated with each. I bet you're spicy."

She took a deep breath. "Do you want me to throw this lemonade at you or not? Because you're really sending a clear message. *I am an asshole. Please throw this drink at me.*"

Norm laughed. "I'd rather not mess up my suit. But you're right, I should be more clear. You have limited options. I originally thought to torture you to find out how much you know. You've already told me you know about our spawning pools, and that's really all I need."

He paused to let that sink in. She was no longer necessary. They could kill her at any time.

"How do you know I haven't shared my knowledge with others?" She hoped she was buying time for a rescue and not roping herself into an interrogation with him.

"If you'd been able to send a signal to the *Arbiter*, the place would be crawling with Sadirians," he said. "And I doubt your friend here let you share anything with other Earthlings."

So much for stalling.

"I could still torture you for the fun of it," he said. "It would be interesting to see how the taste of your blood would change if I killed your partner, since it's obvious you've pair-bonded." He paused and smiled at her, giving her a chance to process just how much power he held.

"Do all Tau Ceti have this kind of flair for the dramatic, or did you pick it up from being on Earth too long? Because, you know what they say—you are who you eat."

Norm laughed. "Oh, I do hope I don't have to kill you. You're one of the more entertaining humans I've encountered."

"I'll be sure to add that to my resume. 'Entertainer for vampire space frogs'."

He laughed again, which was perfect. If she could keep him talking, that would give Brendan time to get to them.

"I'm afraid the only way I can justify keeping you alive is if you prove yourself useful—beyond your wit and tendency toward violence."

"What do you have in mind?"

"If you truly are unwilling to assist with our spawning pools, perhaps you could help out some of our colleagues. We're not the only ones facing challenges in acclimating to Earth. They're loving the cold, but I hear the Centaurans are having trouble adjusting to the oxygen levels in the Himalayas."

She really, really wanted to smash the pitcher into the side of his face. But then they would kill her. And Khel. She still wasn't ready to give up hope that the signal would reach Brendan and he could... She didn't even know. If he was with Khel's commander on the *Arbiter*, surely there would be something they could do.

"Death or cooperation," she said. "Like that's actually a choice."

"I knew I had you pegged as a crusader." Norm shook his head, then grinned and gestured to his goons. She spoke quickly.

"I have some questions before we start working together."

He blinked a few times, then smiled and leaned back in his chair, waving off his lackeys. She had surprised him. Good. She wanted him off-balance...before she put him on *Balance*.

She smiled.

"Well, this is a most pleasant surprise," he said. "What do you need to know?"

Chapter Fourteen

There was no way that Paige was considering collaborating with the Tau Ceti. And the Centaurans? Cygnus X, how had they managed to set up a base on Earth? The problem was so much worse than Khel had thought. And it went beyond this one planet.

The Tau Ceti had learned how to thwart not only the cloak for his ship, but they had shut down all systems—even the failsafe self-destruct. Whatever technology they had developed, it posed a serious threat to the Coalition. Possibly a fatal one. Adding to that the fact that the Tau Ceti were working in concert with others...

Strength in numbers had been on the Coalition's side. They had colonized most of the Milky Way, setting up bases and building new planetary populations. They had fleets of ships and outnumbered any other single species that was allied with them.

And *every* new species discovered allied with them. The Coalition didn't offer a choice.

But if other planets started banding together, if they were making advances like the Tau Ceti had demonstrated... The Coalition didn't stand a chance.

When Adam approached Khel with his plan to try to bring more freedom to Coalition citizens, it had seemed insane. The disruption it would cause to their society… Was nothing compared to what they were truly facing. He still couldn't believe that no one had discovered what was going on.

He could only hope that Paige's panic button was transmitting and that Brendan would pick up its signal. If the Tau Ceti had taken Khel and Paige to their spawning pools, they were far enough from settlements that Adam could order interceptors to the surface. All they needed was more time.

"Tau Ceti and Centaurans," Khel said. "Are there any other Coalition 'allies' here that will face the tribunal?"

Norm laughed. "You'd be surprised how many of us have been unhappy under the Coalition's rule. Even among your own citizens."

Khel couldn't bring himself to respond. His teeth ground together. Earth's planetary liaison working with the Tau Ceti was bad enough. The corruption that had been exposed as Khel dug into his smuggling operation was appalling. And that was before he knew about the Tau Ceti *and Centauran* settlements.

"When was the last time anything changed in the Coalition?" Norm asked. "What you have isn't peace—it's stagnation. Trust me, I come from a planet that's a swamp. I know these things. This is the beginning of the end for the Coalition."

"Yeah, yeah," Paige said. "Let's finish with the posturing."

She lifted her backpack to the table and stood. The guards shifted forward, but Norm gestured for them to stand down again.

"Khel's told me enough about the Coalition that I already know I don't like them. If you guys are setting up shop and willing to let me in, I can at least stop you from totally messing up the planet while you're putting down roots. Especially since it's going to happen no matter what."

She opened her bag and pulled out several empty specimen containers along with the ones holding *Balance*, then said, "Take me to your spawning pools."

Norm smiled and stood. "Excellent. A most reasonable choice."

"I want to keep Khel, though." She turned toward Khel and ran her fingertip along his jaw. "No vaporizing him, no matter how annoying he can be."

Something in her gaze, an intensity that he recognized, told him that it was a ruse—it had to be a ruse. And part of a plan. He trusted her.

She turned back to Norm and said, "I'm assuming you have a lab for me to work in and someone who can explain your technology?"

"Absolutely. But you don't have to get started right

away."

"I'd rather get it over with." She fiddled with her specimen jars and swung her bag over her shoulder. "Make Khel walk out front."

"So my guards can keep him in check?" Norm asked.

Paige shrugged. "I just like watching his ass while he walks, but that, too."

Norm laughed and she smiled. It made Khel's stomach churn. But he believed in her. Believed she had a plan and knew what she was doing.

She had said they underestimated Earthlings and that was their best chance to escape. Walking behind the guards with Norm gave her an opening. And she had the *Balance* in her hands.

Khel glared at them, trying to look betrayed and angry. He barely resisted as the guards turned him around and pushed him forward, listening closely as Paige talked to Norm behind them all.

"My coworkers have always told me it's weird that I never go anywhere without specimen vials. Joke's on them."

Khel could hear her fidgeting, her clothing rustling as she moved.

"Crap. These are already full from that drainage ditch I was testing yesterday. Could you hold this one for me?"

"Certainly," Norm said. "I'm happy to help."

Khel smirked as he imagined Norm taking the small

cylinder. He was sure Paige had figured out a way to get some *Balance* on the outside. He counted down in his mind. *3-2-1.*

Norm's body barely made a sound as it impacted with the soft earth. Khel dropped and kicked out with his legs, sweeping the guards' feet. One leapt clear, but the other was caught and fell.

Jumping back up, Khel struck the one that was still standing. In his periphery, he saw Paige swing her arm, liquid spraying the guard on the ground.

They hadn't had a chance to sound the alarm. If they could take out this last one—

The cyborg dropped its weapon and lifted its arms in the air. That was odd.

Paige's eyes were wide and her mouth had dropped open. Then she smiled and nodded.

"I guess not everyone in the Coalition is too complacent to take action," she said.

Khel looked over his shoulder at *four* interceptors blocking out the sky above the trees. He laughed, relief flooding his body.

Paige opened another vial of *Balance* and splashed the last cyborg, then watched him fall. She nudged all three prone Tau Ceti with her foot and nodded. When she turned to Khel and smiled, his heart started to pound. They had done it.

She stepped over the guards and jumped into his arms,

kissing him passionately. He crushed her to his chest, devouring her mouth with his. She wrapped her legs around his waist, bringing their bodies even closer together.

Three of the interceptors broke away from the group, fanning out over the area. No doubt, they were searching for more Tau Ceti, building a sensor web that would hopefully detect any who tried to escape.

Or they simply couldn't stomach Khel's display of affection. He was amazed to realize that he didn't care.

The voice that projected from the remaining ship's communications relay as it landed was one he recognized, but it wasn't Sadirian.

"Ugh, stop it! That's my sister!"

Paige broke off the kiss and shouted, "Shut up, Brendan!"

She pressed her forehead to Khel's and they laughed.

"Come on," she said, sliding down his body and lacing their fingers together as she stood next to him. A ramp was opening beneath the main interceptor and she pulled him toward it, squeezing his hand. "I want to see where this takes us."

Chapter Fifteen

Two spaceships in one day. Paige could barely believe it. But the interceptor sat in front of her, its chrome hull reflecting the trees around them. The ship had the same sleek lines as Khel's skimmer—before the Tau Ceti had snapped it in pieces—but was a complete circle rather than a half-moon. Panels had unfolded from the bottom of the ship to hold it up off the ground.

Cylindrical mechanisms protruded from the outer ring of the ship at regular intervals. Some rotated around as if they were scanning the area. Others very obviously had weapons attached, the design a larger version of the phase rifles she had seen.

The Sadirians weren't messing around with their interceptors.

She'd probably be more comfortable on board than staring at its guns. Before she could set foot on the ramp, Brendan ran out of the ship. He grabbed her up in a huge bear hug the likes she hadn't experienced since High School.

A dozen people—aliens—marched down the spaceship's ramp after him, carrying phase rifles and stunners. They were all wearing shiny silver one-piece uniforms. The belts at their waists had a few items attached to them of various shapes and sizes. She could only speculate about what they did. Their faces were concealed in featureless chrome helmets, and they wore thick gloves and boots.

Some disappeared into the foliage, while a few remained to deal with the Tau Ceti she and Khel had taken down. She focused on her brother.

"I'm so glad you're okay," he said.

Dammit, her eyes were tearing up. She squeezed him back just as hard, trying to shake it off.

"You think cyborg vampire space frogs can take me down? Please."

He laughed, then set her back on her feet—but he kept one arm around her shoulders. He extended his hand to Khel and said, "Thank you. For keeping her safe."

Khel clasped Brendan's forearm in what must be the Sadirian version of a handshake. He set his other hand on Brendan's shoulder.

"No thanks are required. And in truth, she aided me much more than I aided her. Paige is an incredible warrior." Khel glanced down at her, his cheeks turning pink. "You should also know, we—"

"I shouldn't know anything. I got enough of an eyeful already." Brendan shook his head, clenching his eyes tightly shut for a moment. "What I should have done was warn you. Paige is...outgoing. I thought you'd be immune to her charms. I should have known better."

"Underestimate me at your peril," she said. "And talking about me as if I'm not present will earn you consequences."

She stuck her fingers between a pair of Brendan's ribs where she knew he was incredibly ticklish and he leapt about a foot off the ground.

"Paige!" He rubbed the spot and glared at her.

She grinned, then stepped forward so she could stand next to Khel instead. She tucked herself against his side and wrapped her arm around his waist.

"What are you wearing?" She hadn't noticed before, but Brendan was dressed in a silver catsuit just like the Sadirians. Well, his didn't have the shiny chrome helmet or gloves. The outfit made his red hair look extra coppery.

"You look like something out of a science fiction movie from the 50s," she said.

He glared at her. "It's a Coalition uniform. We have to wear them on the *Arbiter*."

"I look forward to seeing you in one of them." Khel grinned down at her. She could get used to that grin.

"I look forward to seeing you *out* of one." She put her hand on the back of Khel's neck and pulled him close for another kiss.

Brendan groaned in the background.

"I see you're keeping the human safe."

Khel jumped at the booming voice, his body stiffening in ways that weren't nearly as much fun as earlier in the day. He turned to face the trio of people Paige only just realized had been hanging around close by.

One was a man almost as big as Khel, with dark hair and thick stubble covering his jaw. He was flanked by two women—a blonde and a brunette. The brunette was also tall. Her thin, wiry build and ready stance screamed 'soldier'. Definitely Sadirian.

Brendan walked to her side and she reached for his hand without seeming to think about it. Was that Kira? Her new sister-in-law…

Paige would deal with that later.

The blonde, though, was picking at the collar of her uniform and shifting her weight from foot to foot. Her hair was pulled up in a messy bun, and she kept reaching to her face as if she was adjusting invisible glasses, then letting out little sighs. That one had to be human.

"General Serath," Khel said. "I mean Adam. Yes, Paige Sloan is in excellent health."

"Apparently." Adam leveled a stare at them, one eye a rich green and the other a deep blue.

"Whoa, that's a cool design," Paige murmured. "Nice to see you guys are capable of creativity."

"Adam is a gl—"

Khel stopped himself from finishing, and it was a good thing. Paige was pretty sure she could make him jump, too, if he dared to use that word again. The blonde woman was glaring at him as well.

"An unexpected result," Khel said. "What you see is nature, not science."

"I like to think he's a little of both." The blonde woman hooked her arm in the crook of Adam's elbow, and waved at Paige with her free hand. "Greetings, fellow Earthling. I'm Evelyn."

"Hi." Paige smiled at her, then nodded toward the brunette. "I'm guessing that makes you Kira."

Kira nodded curtly. "That's correct."

Paige smiled and cocked her head to the side as she moved her gaze to Brendan. "And that makes you a dead man. Mom's going to go nuts when she finds out you got hitched without telling her."

Brendan shook his head. "Neither of us will be telling her for a while. We have other priorities. Besides, it was important that Kira and I formalize our relationship. Being pair-bonded to an Earthling will give Adam a stronger case for appointing her as the new planetary liaison for Earth and should also help with them recognizing the Department of Homeworld Security."

"The what?"

"Earth's First Contact committee," Kira said. "That's what Brendan's calling it."

Paige snorted. "Of course he is."

Evelyn shrugged. "I don't know. I think it's kind of

catchy."

"So, the three of us get to decide the fate of the planet?" she said.

The idea was insane.

"We're working on that." Kira nodded toward Adam. "Adam still needs to return to Sadr-4 and present the case to the Coalition High Council. Until the First Contact Committee—"

Brendan cleared his throat.

Kira sighed, then said, "Until the Department of Homeworld Security is recognized, they'll continue making all decisions regarding Earth."

Paige's stomach seemed to fall to her feet. Three humans determining the fate of their planet was a hell of a lot better than a bunch of aliens who didn't have any stake in their homeworld—especially given what she knew of their society.

"How likely are they to recognize our sovereignty?" Paige said.

Adam and Kira exchanged a glance. Paige could feel Khel stiffen beside her.

"That bad, huh?"

"We'll do our best," Adam said. "But there are other matters we need to bring to the High Council. The Tau Ceti must be dealt with for exploiting Earth's resources."

Khel shook his head. "It's much worse than that. They weren't just trespassing. They were setting up spawning pools."

Kira's jaw dropped. Adam hid his surprise a bit more effectively, but it was still there.

"Norm—their leader—also told us the Centaurans are here, looking to set up a permanent presence," Paige said. "And they're not the only ones."

Adam wrapped his arm around Evelyn and pulled her against his side.

"General, Earth has not been properly managed." Kira's voice was strong. Whatever shock she had experienced, she was over it, and ready to take action.

Paige liked that.

"There is a very strong case to bring in a First Contact committee at this point, given this information," Kira said.

"Agreed." Adam leveled a stare at Khel again. "If we can prove it. But that proof will also bring the Coalition into the first real war we have experienced in thousands of years."

"The war has already begun," Khel said. "The Tau Ceti were able to completely incapacitate my ship. They've developed new technologies that will bring the Coalition to its knees if we don't stop them."

"That's not possible." Kira stepped forward, her hands curling into fists.

"Anything is possible," Paige said. "All of us standing here together is proof of that."

Khel wrapped his arms around Paige's shoulders,

pulling her against his chest. She let herself lean on him. She had a feeling she'd be doing that a lot in the coming days.

Adam shook his head. "These matters are better discussed aboard the *Arbiter*. Sorca has been dispatched to retrieve the fourth prospective member of the First Contact committee."

"Department of Homeworld Security," Brendan said.

Adam barely glanced at him before continuing. "As soon as she returns with Eric, we can convene the inaugural meeting and determine how to proceed."

Paige wanted to protect her homeworld, but the thought of all those planets stripped bare, their inhabitants left to the mercy of the Coalition... She couldn't let that pass.

She stepped away from Khel, and said, "This has moved beyond the needs of Earth. Whatever we decide, it has to be in the best interest of all the citizens of the Coalition. From what Khel has told me, we have an incredible opportunity to assist your people. If we work together, we can help each other. Maybe repair some of the damage done to other worlds by overharvesting resources."

Adam's lips twitched into an almost-smile. "Brendan was right about you being an excellent candidate for the First Contact Committee."

"Department of Homeworld Security," Brendan said.

Paige rolled her eyes. "We get it, Brendan."

Adam ignored him. "I want to hear more of your ideas for regenerating our stripped planets. Pairing Earth's resources with Coalition technology could go far in easing the transition we will be proposing to the High Council."

A thrill of excitement shot through her. Protecting her world and healing others... Paige was surprised at how much those other planets mattered to her already. She wanted to help. Wanted to do something.

"We have much work ahead of us." Khel moved to stand beside her and took her hand in his.

As long as they kept working together—as partners— she had a feeling everything would be okay. She had to believe it.

With Khel at her side, it wasn't that hard.

She gave him a brief smile. "Then let's get down to business."

Epilogue

Sorca ran through the skimmer's pre-launch sequence for a final time, her mind still buzzing from Vay's cultural indoctrination session. The materials were already blurring, but Sorca didn't care. She just wanted to get planet-side as quickly as possible.

"Sorca."

She turned toward the open hatch at the sound of the familiar voice. Ari was standing to the side of the ramp, his bald head and silver-clad shoulders sticking into the ship due to his formidable height.

"Ari?" she said. "Why are you holding around in the hangar bay?"

"I think you mean, 'hanging around'."

Hanging around? What would he be hanging? But then, 'holding around' didn't make much sense, either.

She shrugged.

"You don't have to go," Ari said.

Sorca let out a sharp laugh. "You heard General Serath's orders. I am to retrieve the Earthling Eric Peterson and bring him back to the *Arbiter*."

"Khel has already been sent to retrieve Brendan's sister.

It makes more sense to send a lower-ranking soldier after Eric."

"Protocols allow for Khel and I to both be off-ship at the same time for important missions. Besides, Serath is back on the *Arbiter*. The command structure is secure."

Ari shook his head. "Earth had a strange effect on Serath. I mean 'Adam'. Until we know why, or the extent of that Earthling's influence on him—"

"*That Earthling* is his bondmate. And her name is Evelyn." Sorca quickly cycled through the last of the checks, then crossed the ship and squatted down next to Ari. "What is this really about?"

"This planet is...unsettling."

That was one word for it. Sorca would have gone with exhilarating, exciting, dangerous, or even *new*. It was a change, and the High Council—along with good soldiers like Ari—viewed change as a threat. So did Sorca.

The difference was, Sorca liked threats. She chose to view them as challenges.

"This planet is primitive and diverse," she said. "Both of those things are uncommon in the Coalition. Steel your nerves and embrace the opportunity."

"Opportunity? For what?"

"For victory!"

She swatted him playfully on the chest. At least, she'd intended to. The force of her "swat" knocked him back hard enough that he hit his head on the hatch. For a moment, he disappeared from her view.

"Apologies." She started to swing herself down over the ramp to reach him more quickly, but he popped back up, rubbing the back of his head.

"I'm okay," Ari said. "This is the exact kind of thing that makes me think perhaps I should go instead."

"The first injury was unintentional. The next will not be."

Ari's gold-hued skin paled at that.

"I mean no offense," he said.

Ari was one of her most trusted security officers, but she would not have him question her abilities. The fact that he was doing so in the first place... Vay must have said something about the cultural indoctrination session. Shared that Sorca's mind was rejecting too much data.

"Your concern for your fellow officers is one of your strengths," Sorca said. "But in this case, it is unnecessary. I assure you, I'm up for the task."

She winked at him, closing both eyes briefly while giving him her most reassuring smile. He opened his mouth as if he was about to speak, but then shut it again and shook his head.

"Of course." He bowed low. "We'll be standing by, just in case you should need anything."

"I know you will." She stepped back into the main area of the ship, then pressed the control that closed the hatch.

Her team would be standing by, but she'd be certain

that she didn't need them. Earth was gloriously unpredictable. For her, that meant fun. But for the others—like Ari—that meant danger she would rather they not face.

They weren't super-strong, extra-resilient, or somewhat immortal—with quirks. Better to keep them on the *Arbiter*, and save this mission for herself.

The space-side doors of the hangar bay opened, revealing a gorgeous view of the planet below. Blue and white and green. For a moment, she was stunned by the simple beauty of it.

The skimmer beeped, reminding her of her mission.

"Eric Peterson," she murmured. "You have no idea what you're in for."

She grinned as she pressed the command to launch.

—

Brendan needs people he can trust in his newly formed Department of Homeworld Security, and there's no one he trusts more than his handler, Eric Peterson. When he asks Adam, aka General Serath, to send someone to bring Eric to the *Arbiter*, Sorca, the head of security is assigned the mission. And when she and Eric meet... Well, it puts a very different spin on alien abduction! Read on for a sneak peek at *Tied up in Customs*.

Tied up in Customs

The Department of Homeworld Security
Book Four

Chapter One

"What is Brendan getting me into now?"

Eric mumbled the words under his breath, scanning the diner as he pretended to read his menu. He made a mental note of the access points of the room—doors, windows— possible lines-of-sight for snipers, items that could hide threats. Everything was cataloged.

Booths lined the seating area, and the central space was filled with a maze of tables. He had asked for a spot near the back wall, where he could easily see all the entrances and exits, as well as the patrons and staff.

The diner didn't use tablecloths, which helped his survey. And it wasn't a place he visited often enough that it would be easy for anyone to predict him being there. Brendan had been very specific that he wanted to meet in this place, but had hedged about why. Which meant he was up to something.

Once, he had roped Eric into being part of a zombie walk. Only once.

Even though Brendan had made Eric swear he would be unarmed when they met, he'd still nearly dislocated a civilian's shoulder trying to protect Brendan from what Eric perceived to be an attack. Brendan had thought it would be okay because zombies "weren't real" and Eric "should have known it was just for fun, since it was his day off…"

For a genius, the guy could be an idiot. Much like Eric was starting to feel.

This was going to be another zombie walk. He just knew it. Especially since Brendan had once again made Eric swear to come unarmed. But if that's what it took to get Brendan back to work on the communications array, so be it.

Honestly, Eric kind of thought Brendan's weirdo play-acting games were…fun. Not that he'd ever admit that to anyone.

Eric was looking forward to this entirely too much. Maybe he did need to take more time off. He could even try to find someone who shared his interests.

Let's see, that would be protecting people, maintaining peace, finding a way to improve everyone's standard of living without compromising what each specific country has achieved, understanding that I'm absolutely dedicated to my job...

At least, he used to be.

He and Brendan had been talking about Eric's single-minded dedication to his job way more than an asset and handler should. Eric chalked it up to building a good rapport with Brendan, but they had come dangerously close to crossing into friend territory.

Crap. They were totally friends.

Eric should ask for a reassignment. Hell, maybe he should retire, like Brendan was threatening to. Find a job in the private sector. With the way his superiors were handling Brendan's project, he might even be able to do more good there.

Eric tossed the menu down on the table just as the door opened. His train of thought stopped when he saw the woman who entered the diner.

Her skin gleamed a rich gold and her dark brown hair fell past her shoulders in thick locks. She was wearing an unbuttoned red-and-black checkered flannel shirt with the sleeves rolled up. Her forearms were corded with muscle.

She had on a nondescript gray T-shirt underneath that was tucked into crisp jeans that hugged equally muscular legs. Her hips and chest looked soft and full, though.

Eric shifted in his seat a bit, his mind already primed to be looking for…something. Even from across the room, he could see that her eyes were pale gray, clear and piercing.

Her gaze landed first on the door to the kitchen, then slid across the open space between the dining area and the chefs, where they handed out food to the wait staff. Her glance briefly paused on the entrance to the hall that led to the bathrooms and again on the rear exit.

She was surveying the room, like Eric had just been doing. She wasn't even trying to be subtle about it, though. Eric leaned back in his chair, resting his hand in his lap for an easier draw—then remembered that he didn't have a weapon.

Shit.

At least he had his handcuffs.

She scanned the crowd, her gaze latching on to his with laser focus. And she smiled.

Eric felt a tightness build in his chest. Not quite dread, but definitely anticipation.

God, she was beautiful.

She started to weave her way toward him, passing waitresses carrying plates filled with eggs and bacon. She stopped suddenly, her eyes going wide as she…sniffed the air. Outright sniffed it, like a hungry animal might.

Beautiful and *strange*.

Eric strained to make out her words through the jumble of noise in the busy diner as she spoke to a waitress.

"What is that?"

The waitress looked irked as she said, "The number seven special."

"Number seven special."

"It's on the menu." When the woman didn't make any sign of moving out of the way, the waitress said, "Do you mind?"

"If I minded your presence, I assure you that you'd know." A near-feral smile twisted the woman's full lips as she watched the waitress back away, then turn and take a different route to her destination.

After a few moments, the woman headed toward Eric again, eyeing the plates of the other customers along the way. She stopped fairly close to him, standing in the empty pathway between the tables, hands at her sides.

It would have been an innocuous pose, except for the way she kept her knees slightly bent and her weight evenly balanced on the balls of her feet—which were encased in black combat boots. From that stance, she could easily spring in any direction she needed.

She held her fingers straight, palms toward him as if she was showing him that she was unarmed. It seemed an almost subconscious gesture, which unnerved him even more.

His gut and his observations told him two things about her right away. She was dangerous and she was not local.

"Eric Peterson," she said.

He waited a few moments before responding, trying to analyze how the situation might play out. He didn't have enough data to form any theories. She obviously knew who he was, so he nodded.

"And you are?"

Her lips twitched up in a mysterious—and somehow taunting—smile.

"Sorca."

"That's it? Just Sorca?"

Instead of elaborating, she lifted her arm and picked at her sleeve. "This is Brendan's shirt. I wear it as proof of my…friendship with him."

What has Brendan roped me into this time?

"And where is Brendan?" Eric asked.

"Elsewhere. He wanted me to tell you that he's safe."

"Why would he feel the need to let me know that?"

"He said you would worry otherwise. I think he was also afraid you might eventually attack me if you were concerned for his safety." She cast that feral smile at Eric, as if the idea delighted her. And waited.

"I'm not… I'm not going to attack you in the middle of a diner," Eric said.

Her face fell. Was she insane? What kind of game was Brendan playing at, and who the hell had he invited to play?

Sorca shrugged, and said, "I am also to give you this."

She started to reach for the pocket on the front of her shirt. Eric's pulse spiked, his body tingling with adrenaline as he prepared to react, thinking of how to protect the civilians in the diner if she should draw a weapon.

Even though he hadn't moved, she froze, fingers extended again in that, "I come in peace" gesture, despite her seeming eagerness to fight. She kept her arms held out to her sides as she leaned forward.

"Perhaps you would feel better if you retrieved the item yourself. It is in the left pocket of Brendan's shirt."

Eric let out a sigh, a small bit of his tension leaving with it. He still kept himself absolutely ready for an attack as he carefully reached two fingers into her pocket for the piece of paper he could see within it. He did his best to ignore the heat from her body or the closeness of his hand to her breast.

He pulled out the note and flicked it open, keeping her in his line of sight. The message was short and unhelpful.

Eric, this is Sorca. I am safe, but our planet is not. Do as she says and she'll bring you to me.
Brendan
P.S. Brown foxes like boxes more than oxes.

Eric would have dismissed it immediately as one of

Brendan's games, except he ended it with one of the codes they had developed for covert communications—an official code meant to let each other know the message was authentic.

Brendan knew he could only use this one once. Why would he waste it on a game?

Talking to Sorca while she was standing next to the table was both awkward and drawing unwanted attention from the nearby patrons. Eric gestured to the empty chair across from him.

"Will you join me?"

One of her dark eyebrows hiked up her forehead. She stared at a plate sitting on a nearby table and licked her upper lip. Slowly.

The tingling coating Eric's skin turned from pre-fight adrenaline to a blasting heat that coalesced in his groin. If this had been part of a regular assignment—part of a mission—things could get very interesting between them. But this was one of Brendan's games. Probably.

Eric shoved away the physical reaction, not letting himself fully register the thoughts that were behind them —thoughts he couldn't seem to stop, at least as long as he was looking at Sorca. Eating would probably help take his mind off of her .

He slid his menu across the table to her as she sat, and said, "What'll you have?"

Her brow furrowed as she looked at the menu, cocking

her head to the side. The smirk vanished from her lips as she studied it—holding it upside-down. Was she pretending that she couldn't read?

With a laugh, she shook her head and tossed the menu back across the table. "Whatever you plan to eat will be fine with me as well."

He flagged down a waitress, and said, "Two number sevens, please."

"Sure thing, handsome." The waitress winked at him before walking away.

"Her eye is spasming," Sorca said. "Is she injured?"

"That was a wink. She's fine."

Sorca's brow furrowed as she stared at him.

"What?" he said.

"You confirmed that you are Eric Peterson."

"I am."

"Then why did that woman call you 'Handsome'?"

"Ouch."

Eric chuckled and Sorca joined in—a few moments late.

Pretending she couldn't read *and* that she didn't understand the word "handsome"? He decided to roll with it.

"It's a descriptive word," he said. "It means she likes how I look."

"How you..." Sorca's brow furrowed again as she glanced around the restaurant before her intense gaze settled back on him. "Your physical appearance. She appreciates your physical appearance."

"That's one way of putting it."

Sorca leaned back in her chair, one eyebrow cocked as she cast her smirk at him. He had never been the subject of a brazen stare before. It was more unsettling than he expected.

He sorted through the rules of the game. Sorca was acting the part of someone unfamiliar with local idioms and customs. There was an odd cadence to her speech—which seemed overly formal—but she didn't have an accent that he could place. In fact, she didn't seem to have any accent at all.

She seemed eager to test herself against him physically. The combat boots and stance warned him not to underestimate her. And the muscles on her arms... He'd never seen such definition on a woman.

Brendan had used one of their codes. Maybe this was some sort of military simulation game? He was heading into dangerous territory by bringing Sorca into it, if she *wasn't* military. She could be someone from an associated project that Eric hadn't met yet...

A strange thrill jolted through him at the thought—half dread, half excitement. He needed more information. And the only way he was going to get it was to play along. He stared across the table at the mysterious woman with the devil-may-care smile.

"You have hair on your face," she said.

He felt his jaw drop open. He snapped it shut, started to speak, then shut his mouth again.

He had training to cover any number of cultural differences. He knew six languages, twenty ways to take down an armed opponent without hurting them, many more ways to do so with...different results. But none of his scenarios, none of his experience, came anywhere close to this woman. The energy she put off was completely alien to him.

"Brendan also has hair on his face," Sorca said. "And another male I know who has been staying in this area for a time. Is this considered handsome?"

Another "male"?

"It depends on your taste," Eric said.

"Hmm. I think I like it." She leaned an elbow on the table, craning her neck to look at the rest of his body. Her gaze heated. "Handsome, indeed."

"Thanks." Under his breath, he added, "I think."

If this was her idea of flirting, it was the strangest, most aggressive conversation he'd ever had.

Flirting... Oh, no.

His stomach sank. Was Brendan trying to set Eric up on a date?

It didn't matter if that's what it was. That was not happening. Even if Sorca was the most gorgeous woman he'd ever seen. Who also gave off an aura of being able to handle herself in a fight. Maybe even combat. She could be *ex*-military…

Her behavior was too bizarre for her to be a foreign operative. But there was definitely something not local about her. Like really not local.

She wasn't among the list of Brendan's eccentric friends that Eric had read about during Brendan's background check. Someone new, then. And this was someone Brendan thought would be a good match for Eric?

That theory seemed to be the most plausible. He would have to find a way to let her down easy.

—

About the Author

USA Today Bestselling author Cassandra Chandler uses her vivid imagination to make the world more interesting, spawning the ideas she turns into her whimsical Science Fiction romcoms and darkly evocative Paranormal and Urban Fantasy Romances. Fast-paced and funny, lighthearted or dark, her stories will introduce you to characters you want to be friends with and worlds where you'd like to build a vacation home.